ANALOG I

Also edited by John W. Campbell

PROLOGUE TO ANALOG

ANALOG I

Edited by
JOHN W. CAMPBELL

DOUBLEDAY & COMPANY, INC.
GARDEN CITY, NEW YORK

All of the characters in this book are fictitious, and any resemblance to actual persons, living or dead, is purely coincidental.

DOUBLEDAY SCIENCE FICTION

To
Lynn and Jim, and many thousand others
who are starting their own expeditions
into the future world—not in fiction, but in life.

CONTENTS

INTRODUCTION

That group of writings which is usually referred to as "mainstream literature" is, actually, a special subgroup of the field of science fiction—for science fiction deals with all places in the Universe, and all times in Eternity, so the literature of here-and-now is, truly, a subset of science fiction.

In many ways, science fiction is a much more difficult type of literature to write; it puts far more severe demands on the author than does the conventional story—partly *because* it is not conventional. It is, many times, the author's aim to communicate to the reader the emotional attitudes entailed in an entirely different set of conventions—a task sometimes beyond the author's abilities, and many times beyond the ability of the average American citizen to grasp. Oriented from birth in a culture that holds certain values as Natural Of Course Truths Beyond Question, a story deliberately based on a culture which holds other truths is going to cause considerable mind-stretching . . . and most modern Americans, as evidenced by the stories found in the mass-media magazines, don't enjoy mind-stretching new viewpoints.

Science fiction is, of course, like any literature—and unlike textbooks, essays, etc.—"for fun," for entertainment.

But . . . what *is* fun?

For some, it's a roller coaster, with the intense fun of being delightfully scared. For some it's the challenge—the real challenge, with very real danger—of mountain climbing, or cave-exploring, which is anything but a spectator sport, and much harder and more dangerous work than you can ordinarily pay people to undertake. For others, fun is lying in the shade of a tree on a summer vacation, and snoozing. Or "fishing" of the type that's an excuse for stretching out near a stream and doing nothing else.

Some like the spectator sports—yelling themselves hoarse watching a team of experts do something tricky and active.

So science fiction is for fun, all right—but basically, it's not the summer-vacation-snooze type of fun. More like the roller-coaster or mountain-climbing type, it presents a real mental challenge. It demands active participation—not spectator type watch - what - those - characters - are - doing. Rock-climbing calls for flexibility, the ability and willingness to stretch muscles, and twist yourself into unusual positions in getting where you are trying to go.

Some science fiction requires an equal flexibility. It's not just a matter of gadgets and new machines—it is, equally, a problem of human attitudes and emotions, some of which seem, at first once-over-lightly, impossible. That *nobody* could believe such things! That *nobody* with an intelligence could accept such attitudes. . . .

So? Well, history shows that the actual range of what-people-can-accept without the slightest trouble is rather more extensive than our current culture acknowledges. It was only about ten generations ago that your own ancestors, lacking TV, movies, and summer theater entertainment, gathered around to watch a witch being burned. And some ten generations earlier, the goodfolk of the town gathered in the public square—holding their children up so they could see better—to watch some rebellious wight being drawn and quartered.

While less than a century ago, young women lost consciousness at the emotional shock of an improper word. And that *wasn't* fakery on their parts—they had genuine beliefs, due to orientation of their culture, so powerful that the emotional shock did cause fainting.

Science fiction does, of course, involve stories based purely on marvelous machines of the future . . . but not always or necessarily in awe-struck wonder at them. "The Hunch," by Christopher Anvil, is certainly a gadget-machine story, but one can scarcely say that the marvelous machines are being viewed with awe-struck wonder.

Actually, probably the most marvelous, complex, and unreliable machine Mankind has ever built is the machinery called "The Law"—and, be it noted, science fiction can have fun with that. Lloyd Biggle did, in "Monument." One thing you can bet on with practically 100 per cent solid assurance is that the legal systems of the future will be more complex, more compartmentalized, and more self-defeating in their aim to achieve Justice than they are today!

You know, when a man takes a vacation, normally he does not work less, be less active, rest more—he works harder, more violently, and goes short on sleep. The fun of a vacation is not ordinarily lessened activity—but a different kind of activity. The postman takes a bus ride through the country, and the bus driver takes a hike through the mountains; the theater owner hires a cruise boat and goes fishing, while the fisherman goes to the theater. Usually, fun and relaxation prove to be doing something different.

That, in essence, is what science fiction offers: something different—and it's strictly an active-participation sport. *You* have to stretch your viewpoints, *you* have to reach for new ideas, and move, for a while, outside your own, familiar orientations of American culture.

And . . . if you think you "know of course" the fundamental attitudes that our Founding Fathers held when the American Culture was being established . . . guess again, friend! Or read "Remember the Alamo!", if you really have the emotional agility and stretch to realize that "American culture" has to be divided into time sections. "Remember the Alamo!" is quite a bitter little piece . . . if you don't realize that what human beings feel is *not* "natural, human emotion" but a product of orientation, as unnatural, in fact, as a peroxide blonde in a synthetic "mink" coat. And "modern" somehow doesn't always seem to come out "better"; personally, I don't find the "modernized versions" of Davy Crockett and Colonel Bowie any improvement at all. . . .

If you don't like that sort of stretching, of course, you can always go back to the narrowly limited confines of modern, mainstream literature, where it isn't considered necessary to suggest that human beings can, and have, experienced really powerful emotions—not petty worries about who's sleeping with who's wife—and can, and have, held deeply and with total dedication, attitudes we cannot believe, today, any human being could hold.

Science fiction is for fun—fun for those who enjoy stretching, reaching beyond the daily limits. If you want to try thinking with new attitudes, if thinking is, for you, fun—then science fiction is fun.

Otherwise, better try something other than this book.

John W. Campbell

ANALOG I

MONUMENT

By Lloyd Biggle, Jr.

It came to O'Brien quite suddenly that he was dying.

He was lying in a sturdy, woven-vine hammock, almost within reach of the flying spray where the waves broke in on the point. The caressing warmth of the sun filtered through the ragged *sao* trees. The shouts of the boys spearing fish off the point reached him fitfully on playful gusts of fragrant wind. A full gourd hung at his elbow. He had been half-dozing in a drowsy state of peaceful contentment when the realization snapped coldly across his idle thoughts and roused him to icy wakefulness.

He was dying.

The fact of death disturbed him less than the realization that he should have thought of it sooner. Death was inevitable from the instant of birth, and O'Brien was a long lifetime from babyhood. He wondered, sometimes, just how old he might be. Certainly a hundred, perhaps even a hundred and fifty. In this dreamy land, where there were no seasons, where the nights were moist and the days warm and sunny, where men measured age by wisdom, it was difficult to keep an alert finger on the elusive pulse of time. It was impossible.

But O'Brien did not need a calendar to tell him he was an old man. The flaming-red hair of his youth had faded

to a rusty gray. His limbs were stiff each morning from
the night's dampness. The solitary hut he had built on the
lovely rise of ground above the point had grown to a sprawl-
ing village, as his sons, and grandsons and great-grandsons,
and now great-great grandsons, brought home their wives.
It was the village of *langru*, the village of fire-topped men,
already famous, already a legend. Maidens were eager to
mate with the young men of fire, whether their hair was red
or the native blond. The sturdiest youths came to court the
daughters of fire, and many of them defied tradition and
settled in the village of their wives.

O'Brien had enjoyed a good life. He knew he had lived
far beyond the years that would have been his in the crazed
rush of a civilized land. But he was dying, and the great
dream that had grown until it shaped his life among these
people was beyond his reach.

He jerked erect, shook his fist at the sky, and shouted
hoarsely in a long-unused language. "What are you waiting
for? What are you waiting for?"

As soon as O'Brien appeared on the beach, a dozen boys
came splashing towards him. "Langri!" they shouted.
"Langri!"

They leaped about him excitedly, holding up fish for his
approval, waving their spears, laughing and shouting.
O'Brien pointed up the beach, where a large dugout canoe
was drawn up on the sand.

"To the Elder," he said.

"Ho! To the Elder! Ho! To the Elder!"

They raced ahead of him, scrambling furiously for places
because the canoe would not hold them all. O'Brien waded
into the melee, restored order, and told off the six he wanted

for paddlers. The others raced into the surf after the canoe, swimming around and under it until the paddlers got up speed.

The boys shouted a song as they dipped their paddles— a serious song, for this was serious business. The Langri wished to see the Elder, and it was their solemn duty to make haste.

O'Brien leaned back wearily and watched the foam dancing under the outriggers. He had little taste for traveling, now that his years were relentlessly overtaking him. It was pleasant to lounge in his hammock with a gourd of fermented fruit juice, acting the part of a venerable oracle, respected, even worshipped. When he was younger he had roamed the length and breadth of this world. He had even built a small sailing boat and sailed completely around it, with the only tangible result being the discovery of a few unlikely islands. He had trekked tirelessly about the lone continent, mapping it and speculating on its resources.

He knew that he was a simple man, a man of action. The natives' awe of his supposedly profound wisdom alarmed and embarrassed him. He found himself called upon to settle complex sociological and economic problems, and because he had seen many civilizations and remembered something of what he had seen, he achieved a commendable success and enjoyed it not at all.

But O'Brien knew that the sure finger of doom was pointing directly at this planet and its people, and he had pondered, and debated with himself on long walks along the sea, and paced his hut through the hours of misty night while he devised stratagems, and finally he was satisfied. He was the one man in the far-flung cosmos who could possibly save this world that he loved, and these people he loved, and he was ready to do it. He could do it, if he lived.

And he was dying.

The afternoon waned and evening came on. Fatigue touched the boys' faces and the singing became strained, but they worked on tirelessly, keeping their rhythm. Miles of coast drifted by, and scores of villages, where people recognized the Langri and crowded the shore to wave.

Dusk was hazing the distant sea and purpling the land when they made the turn into a shallow bay and rode the surf up onto a wide, sloping beach studded with canoes. The boys leaped up and heaved the canoe far up onto the beach. They slumped to the sand in exhaustion, and bounced up a moment later, beaming with pride. They would be guests of honor, tonight, at any hut in the village they chose to visit. Had they not brought the Langri?

They moved through the village in a procession that gained in numbers with each hut they passed. Respectful adults and awed children stepped forth and solemnly followed after O'Brien. The Elder's hut was apart from the others, at the top of the hill, and the Elder stood waiting there, a smile on his wrinkled face, his arms upraised. Ten paces away O'Brien stopped and raised his own arms. The villagers watched silently.

"I greet you," O'Brien said.

"Your greetings are as welcome as yourself."

O'Brien stepped forward, and they clasped hands. This was not a native form of greeting, but O'Brien used it with the older men who were almost life-long friends.

"I ordered a feast in the hope that you would come," the Elder said.

"I came in the hope there would be a feast," O'Brien returned.

With the formalities thus satisfied, the villagers began to drift away, murmuring approval. The Elder took O'Brien's arm and led him past the hut, to a small grove of trees where the hammocks hung. They stood facing each other.

"Many days have passed," the Elder said.

"Many," O'Brien agreed.

He looked at his friend closely. The Elder's tall, gaunt frame seemed as sturdy as ever, but his hair was silvery white. The years had traced lines in his face, and more years had deepened them, and dimmed the brightness in his eyes. Like O'Brien, he was old. He was dying.

They settled themselves in the hammocks, and lay facing each other. A young girl brought gourds to them, and they sipped the drink and rested in silence as the darkness closed in.

"The Langri is no longer a traveler," the Elder said.

"The Langri travels when the need arises," O'Brien said.

"Let us then talk of that need."

"Later. After we have eaten. Or tomorrow—tomorrow would be better."

"Tomorrow, then," the Elder said.

The girl returned with pipes and a glowing coal, and they smoked in silence while fires leaped high in the darkness and the rippling night breeze brought the savory odors of the coming feast blended with the crisp sea air. They finished their pipes and solemnly took their places of honor.

In the morning they walked together along the shore, and seated themselves on a knoll overlooking the sea. Sweet-scented blossoms crowded up around them, nodding in the

2

wind. The morning light sparkled brightly on the leaping water. Brightly-colored sails of the fishing fleet were pinned flower-like to the horizon. To their left, the village rested sleepily on the side of the hill, with only three thin plumes of smoke drifting upwards. Small boys romped in the surf, or walked timidly along the beach to stare up at the Elder and the Langri.

"I am an old man," O'Brien said.

"The oldest of old men," the Elder agreed promptly.

O'Brien smiled wanly. To a native, *old* meant *wise*. The Elder had paid him the highest of compliments, and he felt only frustrated—weary.

"I am an old man," he said again, "and I am dying." The Elder turned quickly.

"No man lives forever," O'Brien said.

"True. And the man who fears death dies of fear."

"My fear is not for myself."

"The Langri has no need to fear for himself. But you spoke of a need."

"Your need. The need of all your people, and of my people."

The Elder nodded slowly. "As always, we listen well when the Langri speaks."

"You remember," O'Brien said, "that I came from afar, and stayed because the ship that brought me could fly no more. I came to this land by chance, because I had lost my way, and because my ship had a serious sickness."

"I remember."

"Others will come. And then others, and then more others. There will be good men and bad, but all will have strange weapons."

"I remember," the Elder said. "I was there when you slew the birds."

"Strange weapons," O'Brien repeated. "Our people will be helpless. The men from the sky will take this land—whatever they want of it. They will take the beaches and even the sea, the mother of life itself. They will push our people back to the hills, where they will not know how to live. They will bring strange sickness to our people, so that entire villages lie in the fire of death. Strangers will fish the waters and swim. There will be huts taller than the tallest trees and the strangers that crowd the beaches will be thicker than the fish that run off the point. Our own people will be no more."

"You know this to be true?"

O'Brien inclined his head. "It will not happen this day, or the next, but it will happen."

"It is a terrible need," the Elder said quietly.

O'Brien inclined his head again. He thought, *This lovely, unspoiled land, this wonderful, generous, beautiful people* . . . A man was so helpless when he was dying.

They sat in silence for a time, two old men in the bright sunshine, waiting for the darkness. O'Brien reached out and plucked the blossoms near him, one at a time, and crushed their fragile whiteness in his hands.

The Elder turned a grave face on O'Brien. "Cannot the Langri prevent this thing?"

"The Langri can prevent it," O'Brien said, "if the men from the sky come this day or the next. If they delay longer, the Langri cannot prevent it, because the Langri is dying."

"Now I understand. The Langri must show us the way."

"The way is strange and difficult."

"We shall do what we must do."

O'Brien shook his head. "The way is difficult. Our people may not be able to follow, or the path the Langri chooses may be the wrong one."

"What does the Langri require?"

O'Brien stood up. "Send the young men to me, four hands at a time. I will choose the ones I need."

"The first will come to you this day."

O'Brien gripped his hand, and moved quickly away. His six great-great grandsons were waiting for him on the beach. They hoisted the sail, for the wind was at their back on the return trip. O'Brien looked back as they moved swiftly out of the bay. The Elder stood motionless on the knoll, hands upraised, as long as O'Brien could see him.

O'Brien did not know the official names of the planet, or even if it had an official name. He was only a dumb mechanic, but a good one, and he had been knocking around in space since he was twelve. He had gotten tired being the bottom rung of everyone's ladder, so he had gotten himself a battered government surplus survey ship, and scraped together some supplies, and given a dispatcher five hundred credits to be looking the other way when he took off.

He had no right to be piloting a spaceship or any other kind of ship, but he'd seen it done enough to think he knew the fundamentals. The ship had a perverse streak that matched his own. He had to exhaust his profanity and kick the control panel a few times before it would settle down and behave itself. Pointing it in the right direction was another matter. Probably any bright high school kid knew more about navigation than he did, and his only support came from an out-of-date "Simplified Astrogation for the Layman." He was lost ninety per cent of the time and only vaguely aware of his whereabouts the other ten per cent, but it didn't matter.

He wanted to see some places that were off the usual space lines, and maybe do a little prospecting, and enjoy being his own boss as long as his supplies lasted. He couldn't stop at any of the regular ports, because the authorities would take one look at his nonexistent license and ground him permanently. But some of the smaller, privately owned ports were always in need of a good mechanic, and he could slip in for a night landing, work a couple of weeks until he'd earned enough to get his ship restocked, and slip back into space without exciting anyone.

He did his prospecting, too, nosing about on dozens of asteroids and moons and small planets that were either undiscovered or forgotten. Quite inexplicably he struck it rich. He stuffed his little ship with platinum ore and started back to civilization to realize his fortune.

As usual he was lost, and he wandered aimlessly through space for a month, conserving his fuel and nursing his worn engines. This planet had seemed his best chance, and it was almost his last chance because a faulty fuel gauge misled him, and he ran out of fuel and crashed on landing.

The natives made him welcome. He became a hero by turning his flaming pistol on a large species of bird that sometimes preyed on children. He used up all of his magazines, but he rendered the bird extinct. He explored the lone continent, and found deposits of coal and some metals —insignificant, but enough to lead the natives immediately into a bronze age. Then he turned to the sea, gave the canoes outriggers and sails, and continued his exploring.

By that time he had lost interest in being rescued. He was the Langri. He had his wives and his children. His village was growing. He could have been the Elder at a relatively young age, but the idea of him, an alien, ruling these people seemed repugnant to him. His refusal enhanced the natives' respect for him. He was happy.

He also began to worry. The planet had such scanty natural resources that no one would be attracted to it by prospective plunder. It had another resource that rendered it priceless.

It was a beautiful world. Its beaches were smooth and sandy, its waters were warm, its climate admirable. To the people of the myriads of harsh worlds whose natural riches attracted large populations, dry worlds, barren worlds, airless worlds, it would be a paradise. Those who could leave their bleak atmosphere domes, or underground caverns, or sand-blown villages for a few days in this sweet-smelling, oxygen rich atmosphere could face their lives with renewed courage.

Luxury hotels would line the beaches. Lesser hotels, boarding houses, cottages would press back into the forest. Millionaires would indulge in spirited bidding for choice stretches of beach on which to locate their mansions. The beaches would be choked with vacationers. Ships would offer relaxing sea cruises. Undersea craft would introduce the vacationers to the fantastically rich marine life. Crowded wharves would harbor fishing boats for hire. Industries would grow up to supply the tourists. It would be a year-round business because the climate was delightful the year around.— A multibillion credit business.

The natives, of course, would be crowded out. Exterminated. There were laws to protect the natives, and an impressive colonial bureau to enforce them, but O'Brien knew too well how such laws worked. The little freebooter

who tried to pick up a few quick credits received a stiff fine
and a prison term. The big-money operators incorporated,
applied for charters, and indulged in a little good-natured
bribery. Then they went after their spoils under the protection of the very laws that were supposed to protect the
natives.

And a century or two later scholars would be bemoaning
the loss of the indigenous population. "They had a splendid
civilization. It's a pity. It really is."

The young men came from all the villages. They swung
lightly down the coast with flashing paddles and rollicking
songs. Twenty at a time they came, tall, bronze, their blond
hair bleached white by their days in the sun. They beached
their canoes along the point, and moved with awed reverence into the presence of the Langri.

His questions startled them. They grappled awkwardly
with strange ideas. They struggled to repeat unutterable
sounds. They underwent tests of strength and endurance.
They came and went, and others took their places, and
finally O'Brien had chosen a hundred.

Back in the forest O'Brien built a new village. He moved
in with his hundred students, and began his teaching. The
days were too few and too short, but they worked from dawn
until darkness, and often far into the night, while the other
natives loyally brought food, and the villages in turn sent
women to prepare it, and the entire people watched and
wondered and waited.

O'Brien taught what he knew, and improvised when he
had to. He taught language and law and science. He taught
economics and sociology and military discipline. He taught
guerrilla warfare and colonial procedure. He taught the

history of the people of the galaxy, and the young natives
sat under the stars at night and stared open-mouthed at the
heavens while O'Brien told of flaming space wars and fantastic creatures and worlds beyond worlds.

The days passed, and became a year, and two years, and
three. The young men brought wives to the village. The
young couples called O'Brien father, and brought their first
born for his blessing. And the teaching went on, and on.

O'Brien's strength waned. The damp nights left him fe-
verish, and his swollen limbs tormented him. But he labored
on, and he began to teach the Plan. He ordered practice
invasion alerts, and his grim seriousness startled the natives
of other villages out of their gay indolence. The Plan slowly
took on form and understanding.

When finally O'Brien was too weak to leave his hammock he gathered the most brilliant youths about him and
the lessons continued.

One bright afternoon O'Brien lost consciousness. He was
carried back to his village, to his favorite grove near the
sea. Word went out along the shore: the Langri is dying.
The Elder came, and the head men of all the villages. They
placed a woven canopy over his hammock, and he lived on
through the night, unconscious and breathing laboriously,
while the natives waited humbly with heads bowed.

It was morning when he opened his eyes. The sea was
lovely in the soft sunlight, but he missed the shouts of the
boys rollicking in the surf. *They know I'm dying*, he thought.

He looked at the saddened faces of the men about him.
"Friends . . ." he said. And then, in a tongue that was
strange to them, he whispered, "before God—before my God
and theirs—I have done my best."

The fire of death leaped high on the beach that night,

and the choked silence of mourning gripped the villages. The next day the hundred young men moved back to their village in the forest to grapple doubtfully with the heritage the Langri had left to them.

II

The *Rirga* was outbound on a routine patrol mission, and Commander Ernst Dillinger was relaxing quietly in his quarters with his robot chess player. He had neatly trapped the robot's queen, and was moving in for the kill when his communication officer interrupted.

He saluted, and handed Dillinger a message. "Confidential," he said.

Dillinger knew from his apologetic manner and the speed with which he made his departure that the news was not good. The man was already closing the door when Dillinger glanced at the message and uncoiled himself in an anguished bellow. The bellow brought him scurrying back.

Dillinger tapped the paper. "This is an order from the sector governor."

"Yes, sir." The communications officer made it sound as if that information was somehow news to him.

"Ships of the fleet do not take orders from bureaucrats and fly-by-night politicians. You will kindly inform his highness that I received my orders from Fleet Headquarters, that I am currently on a third-priority assignment, and that the fact that I am passing through one corner of his alleged territory does not give him automatic control over my movements."

The communications officer fumbled, and produced a notebook. "If you will dictate the message, sir—"

"I just gave you the message. You're a communications officer. Haven't you got enough command of language to tell him to go to hell in a flattering way?"

"I suppose so, sir."

"Do so. And send Lieutenant Protz in here."

The communications officer made a panicky exit.

Lieutenant Protz sauntered in a moment later, met Dillinger's foreboding scowl with a grin, and calmly seated himself.

"What sector are we in, Protz?" Dillinger asked.

"2397," Protz said promptly.

"And how long are we going to be in Sector 2397?"

"Forty-eight hours."

Dillinger slammed down the message. "Too long."

"Some colony in trouble?"

"Worse than that. The sector governor has lost four scratchers."

Protz straightened up and swallowed his grin. "By all that's spaceworthy! Four of them? Look—I have a leave coming up next year. I'm sorry I won't be able to see you through this, but I wouldn't give up that leave if it were a dozen scratchers. You'll just have to find them without me."

"Shut up!" Dillinger snarled. "Not only does this oaf of a governor lose four survey ships at one crack, but he has the insufferable nerve to order me to start looking for them. *Order*, mind you. I'm letting him know that we have a chain-of-command procedure in the space navy, but he'll have time to get through to headquarters and have the order issued there. They'll be happy to oblige, of course, as long as the *Rirga* is in the general area."

Protz reached over and took the paper. "So they send a

battle cruiser to look for four survey ships." He read, and chuckled. "It could be worse. We might find them all in the same place. The 719 turned up missing, so they sent the 1123 to look for it. And then they sent the 572 after the 719 and the 1123, and the 1486 after the 719 and the 1123 and the 572. Lucky thing for them we happened to be here. That nonsense could have gone on indefinitely."

Dillinger nodded. "Seems curious, doesn't it?"

"We can rule out mechanical failure. Those scratchers are dependable, and four of them wouldn't bubble out at the same time. Do you suppose maybe one of these worlds is civilized to the point of primitive space travel, and is picking them off?"

"Possibly," Dillinger said. "But not very likely. Not more than a tenth of the planets in this sector have been surveyed, but the entire sector has been charted, and the fleet used it for training maneuvers a couple of times. If one of these worlds has developed space travel, someone would have noticed it. No—I figure we'll find all four scratchers on one planet. The same trouble that caught the first caught the others. Whether we can do any good remains to be seen. An unsurveyed world can offer some queer kinds of trouble. Go down to the chart room, and see if you can narrow down the search area. We might even be lucky."

Twenty-four hours later Fleet Headquarters made it official, and the *Rirga* altered course. Protz paced the chart room, whistling cheerfully and making deft calculations on a three-dimensional slide rule. A technician was verifying them on a battery of computers, and having trouble keeping up.

Dillinger scowled at the co-ordinates Protz handed to him. "You figure this system is as good a bet as any?"

"Better than any." Protz stepped to the chart. "The 719 last reported in from here, on course—so. There are three possibilities, but only this one is directly on its course. I'd say it's ten to one that this is it. There shouldn't be more than one habitable planet. We can wind this up in a couple of days."

Dillinger snorted. "Only one planet to search for four scratchers! You've been in space too long. Have you forgotten how big a planet is?"

"Like you said, we might be lucky."

They were lucky. There was one habitable planet, with a single, narrow, sub-tropical continent. On their first observation they sighted the four glistening survey ships, parked neatly in a row on a low rise overlooking the sea.

Dillinger studied the observation data, squinted at the film strips, and exploded. "Damn! This will cost us a week, anyway, and those fools have just taken some time off to go fishing."

"We'll have to land," Protz said. "We can't be certain."

Dillinger looked up from the film strips, a faint smile on his face. "Sure we'll land. Take a good look at these. We'll land, and after I kick those scratcher crews in the pants, *I'm* going fishing."

The *Rirga* came ponderously to rest a thousand yards down the shore. There were the inevitable scientific tests. A security unit made a meticulous search of the landing area, and dispatched a squad to investigate the survey ships under cover of the alert *Rirga* gunners. Dillinger strode down the ramp, sniffed the sea breeze hungrily, and headed towards the beach.

Protz came up a moment later. "The scratchers are de-

serted. Looks as if they just walked off and left them."

"We'll have to root them out," Dillinger said. "Notify headquarters."

Protz hurried away.

Dillinger walked slowly back to the *Rirga*. The landing area was being consolidated. Patrols were pushing inland and along the shore. One signaled the discovery of a deserted native village. Dillinger shrugged indifferently, and went to his quarters. He poured himself a drink and stretched out on his bunk, wondering if there was anything on board that would pass for fishing equipment.

Protz's voice snapped out of the intercom. "Commander?"

"I'm relaxing," Dillinger said.

"We've found a native."

"The *Rirga* should be able to cope with one native without harassing its commanding officer."

"Maybe I should say the native found us. He wants to speak to the commanding officer."

Dillinger's reflexes were slow. It was a full ten seconds before he sat up abruptly, spilling his drink.

"He speaks Galactic," Protz said. "They're bringing him in now. What shall we do with him?"

"Set up a tent. I'll receive him with due ceremony."

A short time later, resplendent in a ribbon-decked dress uniform, he hurried down the ramp. The tent had been set up, and an honor guard posted around it. The men were, it seemed to Dillinger, struggling to keep their faces straight. A moment later he understood why. The native was a model of bodily perfection, young, intelligent-looking. He wore only a loin cloth of doubtful manufacture. His red hair was dazzling in the bright sunlight.

Standing before him in full dress uniform, Dillinger saw

the humor of the occasion, and smiled. The native stepped forward, his face serious, his manner confident. He extended his hand. "How do you do. I am Fornri."

"I am Commander Dillinger," Dillinger responded, almost automatically. He stepped ceremoniously aside, and allowed the native to precede him into the tent. Dillinger, and a number of his officers, filed after him.

The native ignored the chairs, and faced Dillinger. "It is my sad duty to inform you that you and the personnel of your ship are under arrest."

Dillinger sat down heavily. He turned to Protz, who grinned and winked. Behind him an officer failed to suppress a chuckle. Because the native had spoken in a firm tone of voice, his words carried beyond the tent. Much whispering and some ill-concealed laughter drifted in to them.

A red-headed native who possessed not so much as a dull spear had calmly walked in and placed the *Rirga* under arrest. It was a gag worth retelling—if anyone would believe it.

Dillinger ignored Protz's wink. "What are the charges?"

The native recited tonelessly, "Landing in a restricted area, willful avoidance of customs and quarantine, failure to land at a proper immigration point with official clearance, suspicion of smuggling, and bearing arms without proper authority. Follow me, please, and I will lead you to your detention area."

Protz was suddenly solemn. "He didn't learn to speak Galactic like that from the scratcher crews," he whispered. "It's only been a month since the first ship was reported missing."

Dillinger whirled on the officers that surrounded him. "You will kindly stop grinning. This is a serious matter."

The grinning stopped.

"You see, you idiots, this man represents civil authority. Unless there are special arrangements to the contrary, military personnel are subject to the laws of any planet which has a central government. If there are several autonomous governments . . ." He turned to the native. "Does this planet have a central government?"

"It does," the native said.

"Do you have the personnel of the survey ships under detention?"

"We do."

"Order all personnel back to the ship," Dillinger said to Protz. He said to the native, "You understand—I'll have to communicate with my superiors about this."

"On two conditions. All weapons which have been brought from the ship are considered confiscated. And no one except yourself will be permitted to return to the ship."

Dillinger turned to Protz. "Have the men stack their arms at a place he designates."

Eight days passed before Dillinger was able to get down to final negotiations. Before the conference started he asked to speak with one of the survey men. Natives brought him into the tent, tanned, robust-looking, wearing a native loin cloth. He grinned sheepishly at Dillinger.

"I'm almost sorry to see you, commander."

"How have you been treated?"

"Perfect. Couldn't ask for better treatment. The food is wonderful. They have a drink that I'll swear is the best thing in the galaxy. They built us some huts on the seashore, and told us where we could go and what we could do, and left us alone. Except for the ones that bring our food, and some fishing boats, we hardly see any natives."

"Three native women apiece, I suppose," Dillinger said dryly.

"Well, no. The women haven't come near us. Otherwise, if you're thinking of naming this planet you can call it Paradise. We've been mostly swimming and spearing fish. You should see the fish in that ocean!"

"You weren't harmed?"

"No. They took us by surprise, and disarmed us, and that was it. Same went for the other ships."

"That's all I want to know," Dillinger said.

The natives led him away, and Dillinger opened the negotiations. He sat on one side of a table, flanked by two of his officers. Fornri and two other young natives faced him across the table.

"I am authorized," Dillinger said, "to accept unconditionally your listing of fines and penalties. Four hundred thousand credits have been transferred to the credit of your government in the Bank of the Galaxy." He passed a credit memo across the table. Fornri accepted it indifferently.

"This planet's status as an independent world will be recognized," Dillinger went on. "Its laws will be respected by the Galactic Federation and enforceable in Federation courts where Federation citizens are involved. We shall furnish your government with a communications center, so that contact with the Federation can be maintained, and ships wishing to land may obtain official permission.

"In return, we shall expect immediate release of personnel, return of equipment, and departure clearance for Federation ships."

"That is satisfactory," Fornri said. "Providing, of course, that the terms of the agreement are in writing."

"It will be taken care of immediately," Dillinger said. He hesitated, feeling a bit uneasy. "You understand—this means that you must return all weapons which you have confiscated, both from the *Rirga* and the survey ships."

"I understand," Fornri said. He smiled. "We are a peaceful people. We do not need weapons."

Dillinger took a deep breath. For some reason he had expected the negotiations to collapse at that point. "Lieutenant Protz," he said, "will you see that the terms are drawn up for signature?"

Protz nodded, and got to his feet.

"One moment," Dillinger said. "There is one thing more. We must have an official name for your planet. What do you call it?"

Fornri seemed puzzled. "Sir?"

"Up to now, you have only been co-ordinates and a number to us. You must have a name. It is probably best that you name your own planet. If you don't, someone else will, and you might not like it. It can be your native name for the planet, or a descriptive term—anything you like."

Fornri hesitated. "Perhaps we should discuss the matter."

"By all means," Dillinger said. "But one word of caution. Once the planet has been named, it will be infernally difficult to change it."

"I understand," Fornri said.

The native withdrew, and Dillinger settled back with a smile, and sipped from a tumbler of the native drink. The drink was everything the survey man had claimed.

Perhaps Paradise would be a good name for the place, he thought. *But then—better to let the natives decide. Para-*

dise might mean something very different to them. All sorts of complications resulted when planets were named by outsiders. He remembered the famous story of the survey ship calling for help from a swamp on a strange planet. "Where are you?" Base had demanded. The survey ship gave its coordinates, and added, quite needlessly, "It's a helluvaplace." The people of that planet had been trying for two centuries to have its name changed, but on all the official charts it was still Hellvaplace.

"Your sun, too," he called after Fornri. "We'll have to name that."

Three hours later they were in space, on their way to Fron, the sector capital. Protz looked back at the dwindling planet, and shook his head. *"Langri.* What do you suppose it means?"

On Fron, Dillinger reported to the sector governor. "So they call it Langri," the governor said. "And—you say they speak Galactic?"

"Speak it rather well, with a kind of provincial accent."

"Easily accounted for, of course. A ship touched down there some time in the past. People liked the place and stayed, maybe. Did you see any traces of such a ship, or ships?"

"No. We didn't see anything except what they wanted us to see."

"Yes. Awkward position you stumbled into. Not your fault, of course. But those survey men . . ." He shook his head. "What beats me is that they learned Galactic. Normally the aliens would learn the native language, unless there was a crowd of them. There is a native language, isn't there?"

"I can't say. I never heard any of them speak anything but

Galactic. Of course I didn't hear them talking among themselves. They withdrew well out of hearing whenever they had to confer about something. But now that I think about it, I did overhear some kids speaking Galactic."

"Interesting," the governor said. "Langri—that must be a native word. I'd better attach a philologist to the staff we'll place there. I'd like to know how they happened to learn Galactic and keep on speaking it, and I'd like to know how long it's been since there were aliens in their midst. Very interesting."

"They're an intelligent people," Dillinger said. "They drove a good bargain, but they were very civilized about it. My orders say I'm to pick up an ambassador for Langri, and the personnel to form a permanent station there. Know anything about that?"

"I'll furnish the personnel for the station. The ambassador has been appointed, and he should be along in a few days. In the meantime, give your men some leave and enjoy yourselves."

A week later H. Harlow Wembling, Ambassador to Langri, waddled up the ramp to the *Rirga,* carrying his ample paunch like a ceremonial badge of honor. He bullied the duty officer, snarled at the crew, and, when Dillinger called at his quarters to pay his respects, demanded a member of the space navy to serve as his valet for the duration of his time on board.

Dillinger emerged wiping his brow, and gave Protz his precise opinion of the new ambassador in words that made the executive officer wince and rub his ears thoughtfully.

"Are you going to give him what he wants?" Protz asked.

"I told him," Dillinger said, still savoring his remarks, "I

told him that the only person on board likely to have that
much free time would be myself, and I lack the proper
qualifications. It's too bad. It's really a shame."

"Oh, we'll be rid of him in no time."

"I was thinking of the natives on Langri. It's politics, of
course. Wembling will be a party stalwart, getting paid off
for years of loyal service and campaign donations. It happens all the time, and most of the appointees are decent
enough. Some of them are even competent, but there's always the exceptional case where a man thinks the word
Ambassador in front of his name elevates him forty degrees
towards divinity. So why does our planet have to draw
this one?"

"It's probably nothing to worry about. These political
appointees never keep their jobs long. Anyway, it's no concern of ours."

"It's my concern," Dillinger said. "I negotiated the Langri
treaty and I feel some responsibility for the place."

They delivered Ambassador Wembling to Langri, along
with the personnel to set up a permanent Federation station.
There was one last-minute altercation with Wembling when
he suddenly insisted that half of the *Rirga's* crew be left
to guard the station. Then they were back in space, ready,
as Dillinger said, to forget Langri and get back to work.

But he did not forget Langri, and there were many times
in the months and years that followed that he found himself reminiscing dreamily of perfect beaches and water
swarming with fish and sea air blended with the perfume of
myriads of flowers. *Now there would be the place for a
vacation,* he would think. *Or for retirement—what a place
that would be for a retired naval officer!*

III

An obsolete freighter, bound from Quiron to Yorlan on a little-used space route, disappeared. Light-years away a bureaucrat with a vivid imagination immediately thought of piracy. Orders went out, and Lieutenant Commander James Vorish, of the battle cruiser *Hiln,* changed course and resigned himself to a monotonous six months of patrolling.

A week later his orders were canceled. He changed course again, and mulled over the development with Lieutenant Robert Smith.

"Someone's been stirring up an indigenous population," Vorish said. "We're to take over, and protect Federation citizens and property."

"Some people never learn," Smith said. "But—*Langri?* Where the devil is Langri? I've never heard of it."

Vorish thought it was the most beautiful place he had ever seen. To the west, that is. Trees stretched glistening pale-green foliage over the narrow beach. Flowers were closing delicately beautiful petals as the evening sun abandoned them. Waves rippled in lazily from an awesomely blue sea.

Behind him, the hideous skeleton of an enormous building under construction stood out sharply in the dusk. The afternoon shift was busily and loudly at work. Clanging sounds and thuds echoed along the shore. Motors chugged and gurgled. Mercifully, the uncertain light disguised the havoc the construction work had wrought in the unspoiled forest.

The man Wembling was still talking. "It is your duty to protect the lives and property of citizens of the Federation."

"Certainly," Vorish said. "Within reason. The installation

you want would take a division of troops and a million credits worth of equipment. And even then it wouldn't be foolproof. You say part of the time the natives come in from the sea. We'd have to ring the entire peninsula."

"They're unprincipled scoundrels," Wembling said. "We have a right to demand protection. I can't keep men on the job if they're in terror of their lives."

"How many men have you lost?"

"Why, none. But that isn't the natives' fault."

"You haven't lost anybody? What about property? Have they been damaging your equipment or supplies?"

"No," Wembling said. "But only because we've been alert. I've had to turn half my crew into a police force."

"We'll see what we can do," Vorish said. "Give me some time to get the feel of the situation, and then I'll talk with you again."

Wembling summoned two burly bodyguards, and hurried away. Vorish strode on along the beach, returned a sentry's salute, and stood looking out to sea.

"There's nobody out in front of us, sir," the sentry said. "The natives—"

He halted abruptly, challenged, and then saluted. Smith came down the slope, nodded at Vorish, and faced west.

"What'd you get?" Vorish asked.

"There's something mighty queer about this situation. These 'raids' Wembling talked about—the natives usually come one at a time, and they don't come armed. They simply sneak in here and get in the way—lie down in front of a machine, or something like that—and the work has to stop until someone carries them away and dumps them back in the forest."

"Have any natives been hurt?"

"No. The men say Wembling is pretty strict about that. It's gotten on the men's nerves because they never know when a native is going to pop up in front of them. They're afraid if one did get hurt the others would come with knives or poison arrows, or some such thing."

"From what I've seen of Wembling, my sympathy is with the natives. But I have my orders. We'll put a line of sentry posts across the peninsula, and distribute some more about the work area. It's the best we can do, and even that will be a strain on our personnel. Some of the specialized ratings are going to howl when we assign them to guard duty."

"No," Smith said. "No, they won't. A couple of hours on this beach are worth eight hours of guard duty. I'll start spotting the sentry posts."

Vorish went back to the *Hiln*, and became the target of an avalanche of messengers. Mr. Wembling would like to know . . . Mr. Wembling suggests . . . If it would not be too much trouble . . . Compliments of Mr. Wembling . . . Mr. Wembling says . . . At your earliest convenience . . . Mr. Wembling's apologies, but . . .

Damn Mr. Wembling! Vorish had been on the point of telling his communications officer to put in a special line to Wembling's office. He breathed a sigh of relief over his narrow escape, and gave a junior officer the full-time assignment of dealing with Wembling's messengers.

Smith strode in out of the darkness from his job of posting the sentries. "Native wants to see you," he said. "I have him outside."

Vorish threw up his hands. "Well, I heard Wembling's side of it. I might as well hear theirs. I hate to ask, but I suppose Wembling will let us have an interpreter."

"He might if he had any, but he hasn't. These natives speak Galactic."

"Now look here." He paused, shook his head. "No, I see you aren't joking. I guess this planet is just different. Bring him in."

The native introduced himself as Fornri, and confidently clasped Vorish's hand. His hair blazed vividly red in the cold glow of the overhead light. He accepted a chair, and sat down calmly. "I understand," he said, "that you are members of the Space Navy of the Galactic Federation of Independent Worlds. Is that correct?"

Vorish stopped staring long enough to acknowledge that it was correct.

"In behalf of my government," Fornri said, "I ask your assistance in repelling invaders of our world."

"The devil!" Smith muttered.

Vorish studied the native's earnest young face before venturing a reply. "These invaders," he said finally. "Are you referring to the construction project?"

"I am," Fornri said.

"Your planet has been classified 3C by the Federation, which places it under the jurisdiction of the Colonial Bureau. Wembling & Company have a charter from the Bureau for their project here. They are hardly to be considered invaders."

Fornri spoke slowly and distinctly. "My government has a treaty with the Galactic Federation of Independent Worlds. The treaty guarantees the independence of Langri, and also guarantees the assistance of the Federation in the event that Langri is invaded from outer space. I am calling

upon the Galactic Federation of Independent Worlds to fulfill its guarantee."

"Let's have the Index," Vorish said to Smith. He took the heavy volume, checked the contents, and found a page headed *Langri*. "Initial survey contact in '84," he said. "Four years ago. Classified 3C in September of '85. No mention of any kind of treaty."

Fornri took a polished tube of wood from his belt, and slipped out a rolled paper. He passed it to Vorish, who unrolled it and smoothed it flat. It was a carefully written copy of an obviously official document. Vorish looked at the date, and turned to the Index. "Dated in June of '84," he said to Smith. "A month and a half after the initial survey contact. It classifies Langri as 5X."

"Genuine?" Smith asked.

"It looks genuine. I don't suppose these people could have made it up. Do you have the original of this document?"

"Yes," Fornri said.

"Of course he wouldn't carry it around with him. Probably doesn't trust us, and I can't blame him."

He passed the paper over to Smith, who scrutinized it carefully and returned it. "It would be a little odd for classification of a new planet to be delayed for a year and a half after the initial survey contact. If this thing is genuine, then Langri was reclassified in '85."

"The Index doesn't say anything about reclassification," Vorish said. He turned to Fornri. "Until we were ordered to this planet, we had never heard of Langri, so of course we know nothing about its classification. Tell us how it happened."

Fornri nodded. He spoke Galactic well, with an accent

3

that Vorish could not quite place. Occasionally he had to pause and grope for a word, but his narrative was clear and concise. He described the coming of survey men, their capture, and the negotiations with the officers of the *Rirga*. What followed brought scowls to their faces.

"Wembling? Wembling was the first ambassador?"

"Yes, sir," Fornri said. "He mocked the authority of our government, insulted our people, and bothered our women. We asked your government to take him away, and it did."

"Probably he has plenty of political pull," Smith said. "He got the planet reclassified, and got himself a charter. Pretty effective revenge for a supposed insult."

"Or maybe he just saw an opportunity to make money here," Vorish said. "Was your government given formal notification of the termination of the treaty and Langri's reclassification?"

"No," Fornri said. "After Wembling there came another ambassador, a Mr. Gorman. He was a good friend of my people. Then a ship came and took him and all of the others away. We were told nothing. Next came Mr. Wembling with many ships and many men. We told him to leave, and he laughed at us and began to build the hotel."

"He's been building for nearly three years," Vorish said. "He isn't getting along very fast."

"We have hired an attorney many worlds away," Fornri said. "Many times he has obtained the conjunction, and made the work stop. But then each time the judge has stopped the conjunction."

"Injunction?" Smith exclaimed. "You mean you've made a lawsuit out of this?"

"Bring Lieutenant Charles in here," Vorish said. Smith

routed the *Hiln's* young legal officer out of bed. With the help of Charles they quizzed Fornri at length on the futile legal action taken by the government of Langri against H. Harlow Wembling.

The story was both amazing and pathetic. The Federation station had taken its communication equipment when it was withdrawn. The natives were helpless when Wembling arrived, and they knew better than to attempt a show of force. Fortunately they had found a friend on Wembling's staff—Fornri wouldn't say whom—and he had managed to put them in touch with an attorney and the attorney had gone to court for them enthusiastically, many times.

He could not intervene in the matter of the violated treaty, because the government had sole jurisdiction there. But he had attacked Wembling's activities on a number of counts, some of which Fornri did not understand. In one instance Wembling had been accused of violating his charter, which gave him exclusive rights to develop Langri's natural resources. Wembling's work on his hotel was halted for months, until a judge ruled that a planet's vacation and resort potential was a natural resource. The natives had just won the most recent round, when a court held Wembling liable for damages because he'd torn down an entire village in clearing ground for the hotel. His charter, the court said, did not permit him to usurp private property. But the damages had been mild, and now Wembling was back at work, and the attorney was trying to think of something else. He was also lobbying to get something done about the broken treaty, but there had been no promise of success there.

"Lawsuits cost money," Vorish observed.

Fornri shrugged. Langri had money. It had four hundred

thousand credits which the Federation had paid to it, and it had the proceeds of a good weight of platinum ore which the friend on Wembling's staff had managed to smuggle out for them.

"There's platinum on Langri?" Vorish asked.

"It didn't come from Langri," Fornri said.

Vorish drummed impatiently on his desk. The Langri situation involved several noteworthy mysteries, but just for a start he'd like to know how the natives had happened to be speaking Galactic when the first survey men arrived. And then—platinum ore that didn't come from Langri. He shook his head. "I don't think you'll ever defeat Wembling in court. You may give him a few temporary setbacks, but in the long run he'll win out. And he'll ruin you. Men like him have too much influence, and all the financial backing they need."

"The conjunctions give us time," Fornri said. "Time is what we need—time for the Plan."

Vorish looked doubtfully at Smith. "What do you think?"

"I think we're obligated to make a full report on this. The treaty was negotiated by naval officers. Naval Headquarters should be filled in on what's happened."

"Yes. We should send them a copy of this—but a copy of a copy may not swing much weight. And the natives probably won't want to turn loose the original." He turned to Fornri. "I'm going to send Lieutenant Smith with you. He will bring a couple of men along. None of them will be armed. Take them wherever you like, and guard them any way you like, but they must make their own photographs of the treaty before we can help you."

Fornri considered the matter briefly, and agreed. Vorish sent Smith off with two technicians and their equipment, and settled down to compose a report. He was interrupted by a young ensign who gulped, flushed crimson, and stammered, "Excuse me, sir. But Mr. Wembling—"

"What now?" Vorish said resignedly.

"Mr. Wembling wants sentry post number thirty-two moved. The lights are interfering with his sleep."

In the morning Vorish strolled around the project to take a good look at Wembling's embryo hotel. Wembling joined him, wearing a revoltingly-patterned short-sleeved shirt and shorts. His arms and legs were crisply tanned, his face pale under an outlandish sun helmet.

"A thousand accommodations," Wembling said. "Most of them will be suites. There'll be a big pool on the terrace overlooking the beach. Some people can't stand salt water, you know. I have the men laying out a golf course. There'll be two main dining rooms and half a dozen small ones that will specialize in food from famous places. I'll have a whole fleet of boats to take people fishing. I might even have a submarine or two—those jobs with rows of observation ports. You might not believe it, but there are hundreds of worlds where people have never seen an ocean. Why, there are worlds where people don't even have water to bathe in. They have to use chemicals. If some of those people can come to Langri, and live a little, now and then, a lot of head doctors are going to be out of work. This project of mine is nothing but a service to humanity."

"Is that so?" Vorish murmured. "I wasn't aware that yours was a nonprofit organization."

"Huh? Of course I'll make a profit. A darned good profit. What's wrong with that?"

"From what I've seen of your hotel, the only minds you'll

be saving will be those of the poor, broken-down millionaires."

Wembling indulged in a grandiose gesture. "Just a beginning. Have to put the thing on a sound financial basis
right from the start, you know. But there'll be plenty of room
for the little fellows. Not in water-front hotels, but there'll
be community beaches, and hotels with rights of access, and
all that sort of thing. My staff has it all worked out."

"It's just that I'm trained to look at things differently,"
Vorish said. "We in the Space Navy devote our lives to the
protection of humanity, but if you'll look at the current
pay scale you'll see that there's no profit motive."

"There's nothing wrong with taking a profit. Where
would the human race be today if nobody wanted a profit?
We'd be living in grass huts back on old Terra, just like
these Langri natives. There's a good example of a nonprofit
society. I suppose you'd like that."

"It doesn't look so bad to me," Vorish murmured.

But Wembling did not hear him. He whirled and darted
away, sputtering an unbelievably pungent profanity. A native, dashing in from nowhere, had attached himself to a
girder that was about to be swung aloft. Workmen were
valiantly striving to remove him—gently. The native clung
stubbornly. Work stopped until he was pried loose and
carried away.

Lieutenant Smith came up in time to see the drama
carried to its comical conclusion.

"What do they expect to gain?" Vorish said.

"Time," Smith said. "Didn't you hear what that native
said? They need time for the Plan—whatever that means."

"Maybe they're planning some kind of a massive upris-
ing."

"I doubt it. They seem to be essentially a peaceful people."

"I wish them luck," Vorish said. "This Wembling is a tough customer. He's a self-activated power unit. I wonder how his weight holds up, the way he tears around keeping things humming."

"Maybe he eats all night. Want to look over the sentry layout?"

They turned away. In the distance they heard Wembling, his voice high-pitched with excitement, getting the work going again. A moment later he caught up with them and walked jauntily along beside Vorish.

"If you'd put in the kind of defense line I want," he said, "I wouldn't have that trouble."

Vorish did not reply. It was obvious that Wembling was going out of his way to avoid injuring the natives, but Vorish doubted that his motives were humanitarian. Inept handling of the native problem might embarrass him in some future court test.

On the other hand, Wembling was not worried in the least about the Space Navy's injuring the natives. The blame for that action could not possibly fall upon him. He had demanded that Vorish erect an electronic barrier that would incinerate any native attempting to pass.

"At the very worst," Vorish said, "the natives are only a minor nuisance."

"They haven't got much for weapons," Wembling said. "But they have enough to cut throats, and there's a hell of a lot of natives in this place if they all decide to come at me at once. And then, their mucking about the project is slowing things down. I want 'em kept out."

"I don't think your throat is in danger, but we'll do what we can to keep them out."

"Guess I can't ask more than that," Wembling said. He chuckled good-naturedly, and looped his arm through Vorish's.

Smith had sited his sentry posts to make a shrewd use of the infrequent irregularities in terrain. He had men at work now, clearing the ground for better visibility. Wembling sauntered along reviewing the results with the casual aloofness of an Admiral of the Fleet. Suddenly he pulled Vorish to a halt.

"This defense line of ours. We'll have to move it."

Vorish regarded him coldly. "Why?"

"In the next two or three weeks we're going to start work on the golf course. We wouldn't be able to get more than half of it this side of the line. Maybe not that much. So we'll have to move it. It wouldn't be safe to have my men working off by themselves. But there's no hurry—tomorrow will do."

"Supposing you tell me what you have in mind," Vorish said.

Wembling summoned a survey party, and they set out under the watchful eyes of a military escort. They moved west along the peninsula, which widened sharply until it became a part of the mainland. They pushed their way through the trees as the perspiring Wembling, enjoying himself immensely, gestured and talked his way around the prospective golf course.

An hour later Vorish took another look at the acreage the golf course was to occupy, and gave Wembling a flat refusal. "The line would be too long here," he said. "I wouldn't have enough men."

Wembling grinned. "The commander is always pulling my leg. You've got plenty of men. They're all down there on the beach."

"My men are working in shifts, just as yours are. If I put those men on guard duty, I won't have any relief for them."

"We both know you could set up an impassable defense that wouldn't require any men," Wembling said.

"We both know I'm not going to do it. Your men can work without naval protection. They'll be safe."

"All right. If that's the way you want it. But if anything happens to them—"

"There's one more thing," Vorish said. "What are you going to do about that abandoned native village where the eighth hole is supposed to be?"

Wembling gazed contemptuously at the distant huts. "Tear it down. Nobody lives there."

"You can't do that," Vorish said. "It's native property. You'll have to get permission."

"Whose permission?"

"The natives' permission."

Wembling threw back his head, and laughed uproariously. "Let 'em take it to court, if they want to waste their money. That last case must have cost 'em close to a hundred thousand, and know what their damages were? Seven hundred and fifty credits. The sooner they use up their money, the sooner they stop bothering me."

"My orders call for the protection of natives and native property just as I protect you and your property," Vorish said. "The natives won't stop you, but I will."

He strode away without looking back. He was in a hurry to get to his office on the *Hiln,* and have a talk with Lieutenant Charles. There was something he remembered reading, a long time ago, in his little-used manual of military government . . .

The days drifted by pleasantly, ruffled only by Wembling's violent protests whenever a native slipped through to slow down construction. Vorish kept an alert eye on Wembling's Operation Golf Course, and waited impatiently for some official reaction to his report on the Langri treaty.

Official reaction there was none, but Wembling's workcrew steadily sliced its way back into the forest. Trees were being hauled away to be cut into lumber. The delicately-speckled grain would make an exquisite and novel paneling for the hotel's interior.

The crew reached the deserted native village and worked completely around it. They made no effort to trespass, though Vorish saw them casting nervous glances in that direction from time to time, as though they hoped it would go away.

Making his morning rounds of the sentry posts, Vorish paused occasionally to turn his binoculars on the work around the village.

"You're sticking your neck out," Smith said. "I hope you realize that."

Vorish made no reply. He had his own opinion of naval officers who were unduly concerned for their necks. "There's Wembling," he said.

With his bodyguards panting on his heels, Wembling was moving at his usual fast pace across the cleared ground. His foreman came forward to meet him. Wembling spoke briefly, and pointed. The foreman turned to his men, and pointed. A moment later the first hut was overturned.

"Let's go," said Vorish.

Smith signaled a squad of navy men into action, and hurried after him. The men reached the village first, and cleared out Wembling's men. Wembling was frozen in impotent rage when Vorish arrived.

Vorish paused to study the row of toppled huts. "Did you have permission from the natives to do this?" he asked.

"Hell, no," Wembling said. "I've got a charter. What can they do about it?"

"Place these men under arrest," Vorish said, and turned away.

Somewhat to his surprise, Wembling said nothing. His aspect was that of a man thinking deeply.

Vorish confined Wembling to his tent, under arrest. He halted all work on the hotel. Then he forwarded a complete report on the incident to Naval Headquarters, and sat back to await results.

The indifference of headquarters to his Langri report had intrigued him. Had someone filed it away as unimportant, or was there a corrupt conspiracy high up in the government? Either way, injustice was being done. The natives wanted time for something they called the Plan. Vorish wanted time to call someone's attention to what was going on. It would be a shame to allow Wembling to finish his hotel while the report on the Langri situation lay in an underling's desk drawer.

With Wembling under arrest and the work stopped, Vorish watched in amusement while Wembling got off frantic messages to exalted persons high up in the Federation government.

"Now," Vorish told himself with satisfaction, "let's see them ignore Langri this time."

The days had added up to three weeks when Headquarters suddenly broke the silence. The battle cruiser *Bolar* was being dispatched, under Admiral Corning. The admiral would make an on-the-spot investigation.

"It doesn't sound as if you're being relieved," Smith said. "Do you know Corning?"

"I've served under him several times, at various places and ranks. You might call him an old friend."

"That's fortunate for you."

"It could be worse," Vorish admitted. He felt that he'd covered himself well, and Corning, even though he was crusty, temperamental and a stickler for accuracy, would not go out of his way to make trouble for a friend.

Vorish turned out an honor guard for the admiral, and received him with full ceremony. Corning stepped briskly down the ramp from the *Bolar* and glanced about approvingly.

"Glad to see you, Jim," he said, his eyes on one of Langri's inviting beaches. "Nice place here. Nice place." He turned to Vorish, and studied his tanned face. "And you've been making good use of it. You've put on weight."

"You've lost weight," Vorish said.

"Always was skinny," Corning said. "I make up for it in height. Did I ever tell you about the time—" He glanced at the circle of respectfully attentive officers, and dropped his voice. "Let's go where we can talk."

Vorish dismissed his men, and took Corning to his office

in the *Hiln*. The admiral said nothing along the way, but his sharp eyes surveyed Vorish's defense arrangements, and he clucked his tongue softly.

"Jim," Corning said, as Vorish closed the door, "just what is going on here?"

"I want to give you some background," Vorish said, and told him about the treaty and its violation. Corning listened intently, muttering an occasional "Damn!"

"You mean they took no official action on it at all?" he demanded.

"That's exactly what they did."

"Damn! Sooner or later somebody's head will roll over that. But it'll probably be the wrong head, and that treaty really has nothing to do with this mess you've gotten yourself into. Not officially, anyway, because officially the treaty doesn't exist. Now what's this nonsense about a few native huts?"

Vorish smiled. He felt that he was on firm ground there —he'd had a long conference with Fornri, exploring all of the angles. "According to my orders," he said, "I'm an impartial referee here. I'm to protect Federation citizens and property, but I am also to protect the natives against any infringements upon their customs, means of livelihood, and so on. Paragraph seven."

"I've read it."

"The idea is that if the natives are treated properly, Federation citizens and property are a lot less likely to need protection. That particular native village is more than just a collection of empty huts. It seems to have some religious significance to the natives. They call it the Teacher's Village, or some such thing."

"Teacher or leader," Corning said. "Sometimes they're the same thing to primitive peoples. That might make the village a kind of shrine. I take it that this Wembling busted right in and started tearing the place apart."

"That's what he did."

"And you warned him ahead of time that he should get the natives' permission, and he laughed it off. All right. Your conduct was not only proper, there—it was commendable. But why did you have to close the whole works down? You could have protected that village, and made him put his golf course somewhere else, and he would have screamed to high heaven without getting anything but laughed at. But you had to stop everything. Were you *trying* to get fired? You've cost Wembling a lot of time and a lot of money, and now he has a real grievance. And he's got plenty of influence."

"It isn't my fault if he wasted time and money," Vorish said. "I advised headquarters of my action immediately. They could have reversed that order any time they chose."

"That's just it. They didn't dare, because there was always the chance that things might blow up. They didn't know the situation here. You caused a pretty stew at headquarters. Why did you arrest Wembling, and keep him in his tent under guard?"

"For his own protection. He'd defiled a sacred place, and I'd be responsible if anything happened to him."

For the first time Corning smiled. "So that's the line. Not bad. It all comes down to a matter of judgment, and that makes it your opinion against Wembling's. You flip your coin and you take your choice, and no one who wasn't on the spot is entitled to vote." He nodded. "I'll follow that up in my report. Wembling stepped out of line. Definitely. The

consequences might have been serious. I can't rightly say that your action was too drastic, because I wasn't here at the time. I don't exactly see what you were trying to do, or maybe I do, but I'll back you up as much as I can. I guess I can keep you from being shot."

"Oh," Vorish said. "So they were going to shoot me. I wondered."

"They were . . . they are . . . going to do their worst." Corning looked steadily at Vorish. "I don't much like it, but I have my orders. You'll return to Galaxia on the *Hiln*, under arrest—to stand court-martial. Personally I don't think you have much to worry about. I can't see them going ahead with it, but right now they think they want to try."

"I won't worry," Vorish said. "I've studied this thing through pretty carefully. I rather hope they try, though. I'll insist on a public court-martial, of course, and . . . but I'm afraid they won't do it. Anyway, I'm glad I'll be leaving Langri in capable hands."

"Not my hands," Corning said. "Not for long. The 984th Squadron is on its way now, to take over. Eleven ships. They're not taking any chance on this thing getting out of hand. The commander is Ernst Dillinger—just made admiral a few months ago. Know him?"

IV

The fishing boat was still in position, far out. Dillinger raised his binoculars, lowered them. As far as he could see, the natives were—fishing. He returned to his desk and sat gazing seaward at the fleck of color that was the sail.

The plush spaciousness of his office annoyed him. It was only his second day in the quarters Wembling had persuaded him to occupy in the completed wing of Hotel Langri, and he was spending most of his time pacing in out-sized circles about the work that piled up on his desk.

He was worried about the natives. He was worried about an enigmatic something or other which they called the Plan, and which they intimated would eventually sweep Wembling and his workers and his hotels right off the planet.

With Hotel Langri opening for business in a few months, and work already beginning on two other hotels, Dillinger knew that the legal expulsion of Wembling had become a flat impossibility. So what were the natives planning? Illegal expulsion? The use of force? With a squadron of the Space Navy standing by?

He got to his feet again and walked over to the curved expanse of tinted plastic that formed the window. The fishing boat was still there. Every day it was there. But perhaps, as Protz suggested, the water off the point was merely a good place to fish.

His intercom clicked. "Mr. Wembling, sir."

"Send him in," Dillinger said, and turned towards the door.

Wembling entered jauntily, hand outstretched. "Morning, Ernie."

"Good morning, Howard," Dillinger said, blinking at Wembling's ridiculously patterned shirt.

"Come down to the lounge for a drink?"

Dillinger lifted a stack of papers from his desk, and dropped it. "Sure."

They walked down a palatial corridor to the lounge, and a uniformed attendant took their orders and brought the drinks. Dillinger idly stirred the ice in his glass and looked through the enormous window at the terrace, and the beach beyond. Wembling's landscaping crew had done its work well. Velvety grass and colorful shrubs surrounded the hotel. The pool, ready for use, stood deserted. Off-duty navy men and workers crowded the beach, and speared fish off the point.

Wembling prated enthusiastically over the progress he was making on his new sites, which were fifty miles down the coast in both directions.

"It's a headache to me, your scattering these sites all over the place," Dillinger said. "I have to guard them."

Wembling reached over and patted his arm. "You're doing a good job, Ernie. We haven't had any trouble since you took over. I'm putting in a good word for you where it'll do the most good."

"There's room for fifty hotels right here on the peninsula," Dillinger said. "Not to mention a few golf courses."

Wembling turned a veiled smile in his direction. "Politics and law," he murmured. "Stay away from both of them, Ernie. You have brains and talent, but it isn't that kind of brains and talent."

Dillinger flushed, and turned his gaze to the window again. The fishing boat was a mere speck on the horizon. It was probably drifting or sailing slowly, but it seemed motionless.

"Have you heard anything about Commander Vorish?" Wembling asked.

"The last I heard, he'd taken the *Hiln* on training maneuvers."

"Then—they didn't fire him?"

"They investigated him," Dillinger said with a grin. "But all he got was a commendation for handling himself well in a difficult situation. My guess is that any action against

him would have resulted in publicity, and someone didn't
want publicity. Of course I don't know anything about
politics and law. Did you want Vorish fired?"

Wembling shook his head thoughtfully. "No. I had no
grudge against him. There's no profit in grudges. We both
had a job to do, but he went at his the wrong way. All I
wanted was to get on with the work, and after he left I
passed the word along to go easy on him. But I thought
they'd kick him out of the navy, and if they did I wanted
him back here on Langri. I think he understood these
natives, and I can always use a man like that. I told him to
get in touch with my Galaxia Office, and they'd make arrangements to get him back here. But I never heard from
him."

"He didn't get fired. The next time you see him he'll
probably be an admiral."

"The same goes for you," Wembling said. "If you ever
leave the navy, come back to Langri. I'm going to have a
big enterprise to run here, and I'll need all the good men
I can get. And good men aren't always easy to find."

Dillinger turned aside to hide his smile. "Thanks. I'll
remember that."

Wembling slapped the table, and pushed himself erect.
"Well, back to work. Chess tonight?"

"Better make it late," Dillinger said. "I've got to get that
work cleaned up."

He watched Wembling waddle away. He had to admire
the man. Even if he loathed him, and loathed his methods,
he had to admire him. He got things done.

Protz was waiting for him when he got back to his office
—Commander Protz, now, Captain of the *Rirga*, the flag

ship of Dillinger's 984th Squadron. Dillinger nodded at him, and spoke into his intercom.

"I don't want to be disturbed." He switched it off, and turned to Protz. "What's the score."

"We're losing," Protz said. "It definitely didn't crash. According to the sentry, it came in for a perfect landing back in the forest. Wembling isn't missing a supply ship, and we know it didn't belong to us. The recon planes have been taking the tops out of the trees in that area, and they can't spot a thing."

"So it wasn't Wembling's," Dillinger said. Since he'd gotten the first report on the unidentified ship, at dawn that morning, he'd been thinking that it had to be Wembling's. He turned in his chair, and looked out to sea. "So the natives have visitors."

"Whoever it was, they were expected," Protz said. "They got the ship camouflaged in a hurry. Maybe they had a landing pit dug there."

"Wembling thinks someone in his supply fleet has been keeping the natives in touch with that attorney of theirs. I suppose we should have monitored the planet. But we'd have to leave a ship in orbit, and we've needed every man, with Wembling building hotels all over the place. Well, the ship is here. The question now, is—what is it doing?"

"Smuggling arms?"

"Just what we need to make this assignment interesting. Has Intelligence turned up anything?"

"Nothing up to 0800 this morning. Want to make a ground search for the ship?"

"It would take too many men. If they have a landing pit, even a ground search might miss it—and we'd be too late now if we did find it. They'll have it unloaded. No. Let

Intelligence work on it, and give them more men if they
think they can use them."

"Anything else?"

"Get ready for the worst. Protz, of all the jobs the navy
has given me to do, this one is the dirtiest. I hoped I'd get
out of it without a shot fired at the natives. I'd much rather
shoot Wembling."

The thing had been mishandled from the start, Dillinger
thought. This attorney the natives had gotten ahold of was
probably competent enough—even Wembling admitted that.
He'd caused Wembling some trouble, but Wembling was
putting the finishing touches on Hotel Langri just the same.

Wembling's chief weapon was political pull. Politics
should be fought with politics, with public opinion, and not
in a court of law. He'd tried to explain that, once, to Fornri,
but the native seemed uninterested. The Plan, Fornri said,
would take care of everything. He did not seem to realize
that it was already too late.

If Dillinger had known in time what was happening to
Langri, he believed he could have stopped it. Documented
information, furnished anonymously to the wealthy ethno-
logical foundations, to opposition newspapers on key
planets, to opposition leaders in the Federation Congress—
the resultant explosion would have rocked the government
and rocked Wembling right off Langri.

But he had not known until he reported to Admiral
Corning and assumed command on Langri. Then he had
done what he could. He had prepared a hundred copies of
a statement on the Langri situation, and accompanied each
with a photo of the original treaty. But he did not dare en-
trust them to normal communication channels, and he had

to wait until one of his officers went on leave to get them on their way. They had probably reached their destinations by this time, and they would be studied and investigated, and eventually there would be some action. But it was too late. Wembling would have most of what he wanted, and probably other vultures, armed with charters, would be coming to the plunder of Langri.

It was tough on the natives. Wembling's men were eating a lot of fresh fish, and the natives' fishing boats had all but vanished from the sites where Wembling was working. Langri had a big native population—too big, and most of its food came from the sea. The word was that the natives weren't getting enough to eat.

Late in the afternoon, Dillinger called Wembling. "You have men flying back and forth all the time," he said. "Have they noticed any unusual native activity?"

"I didn't hear about any," Wembling said. "Want me to check?"

"I wish you would."

"Hold on a minute."

He heard Wembling snapping out an order. A moment later, he said to Dillinger, "Do you think the natives are up to something?"

"I know they are, but I can't figure out what it is."

"You'll handle them," Wembling said confidently. "There was a time when I wanted them annihilated, but since you've been keeping them out of my hair, I'd just as soon live and let live. Hell, they might even be a tourist attraction when I get things going here. Maybe they weave baskets, or carve voodoo charms, or something like that. I'll sell them in the hotel lobby."

"I'm not worrying about their basket weaving," Dillinger said dryly.

"Anyway . . . just a moment. Ernie? Nobody saw anything unusual."

"Thanks. I'm afraid I'll have to call off that chess game. I'll be busy."

"Too bad. Tomorrow night, then?"

"We'll see."

Langri would have been enchanting by moonlight, but there was no moon. Wembling had a scheme to produce artificial moonlight, but until he put it into operation night would smother the planet's beauty in blackness.

Looking down into the blackness, Dillinger saw light. At every native village there were dozens of fires. Often their outlines blurred together into one brilliant patch of light. When they were farther apart, they appeared as a multitude of bright dots leaping up into the darkness.

"You say it isn't normal?" Dillinger asked the recon pilot.

"Definitely not, sir. They fix their evening meal along about dark, when the fishing boats get in. When that's over with, you can fly the whole coast without seeing a flash of light. Except where our men are. I've never seen even one fire going this late."

"It's a pity we know so little about these natives," Dillinger said. "The only one I've ever talked with is this Fornri, and there's always something—distant about him. I never know what he's thinking. Colonial Bureau should have sent a team to study them. They could use some help, too. Their fishing will fall off even more when Wembling gets a mob of tourists out on the water. They'll need some agriculture. What do you make of it, Protz?"

"It's suggestive, but darned if I know what it suggests."

"I know what it suggests," Dillinger said. "A strange ship lands this morning, and tonight every native on the planet stays up all night. They're getting ready for something. We'd better get back and make a few preparations of our own."

There was little that he could do. He had a defense line around each of Wembling's three building sites. He had his ships sited to give maximum support. All that had been worked out months before. He placed his entire command on alert, doubled the guard on the beaches, and set up mobile reserves. He wished he had a few army officers to help out. He'd spent his entire adult life learning how to wage war in space, and now for the first time in his military career he was faced with the possibility of battle, and he was landbound, and in danger of being embarrassed by hordes of untrained natives.

The night intelligence sheet arrived at dawn, virtually blank. Except for the fires there was nothing to report. Dillinger passed it across to Protz, who glanced at it and passed it back.

"Go down and see Wembling," Dillinger said. "Tell him to give his men the day off, and keep them in their quarters. I don't want to see one of them around. That goes for him, too."

"He'll howl."

"He'd better not howl to me. If we knew these natives better, maybe we could see this thing from their point-of-view. Somehow I just can't see them hitting us with an armed attack. It'd get a lot of them killed, and it wouldn't accomplish a thing. Surely they know that as well as we do. Now if you were a native, and you wanted to stop Wembling's work, what would you do?"

"I'd kill Wembling."

Dillinger slapped his desk disgustedly. "O.K. Give him an armed guard."

"What would you do?"

"I'd plant some kind of explosive at carefully chosen points in the hotels. If it didn't stop the project altogether, it'd throw an awful delay at Wembling's grand opening. You know—"

"That might be it," Protz said. "It makes more sense than an all-out attack. I'll put special guard details around the buildings."

Dillinger rose and went to the window. Dawn was touching Langri with its usual lavish beauty. The sea was calmly blue under the rising sun. Off the point . . .

Dillinger swore softly.

"What's the matter?" Protz said.

"Look." Dillinger pointed out to sea.

"I don't see anything."

"Where's the fishing boat?"

"It isn't there."

"Every day as long as we've been on this planet there's been a fishing boat working off the point. Get the recon planes out. Something is decidedly fishy."

Thirty minutes later they had their report. Every fishing boat on Langri was beached. The natives were taking the day off.

"They seem to be congregating in the largest villages," the intelligence officer said. "A7—that's Fornri's village, you know—has the biggest crowd. And then B9, D4, F12—all along the coast. There are fires all over the place."

Dillinger studied a photo map, and the officer circled the

villages as he called them off. "At this point," Dillinger said, "there's just one thing we can do. We'll go over and have a little talk with Fornri."

"How many men do you want?" Protz asked.

"Just you and I. And a pilot."

They slanted down to a perfect landing in the soft sand of the beach. The pilot stayed with the plane, and Dillinger and Protz climbed the slope to the village, making their way through throngs of natives. Dillinger's embarrassment increased with each forward step. There was no sign of a sinister conspiracy. A holiday atmosphere prevailed, the gaily dressed natives laughing and singing around the fires—singing in Galactic, an accomplishment that never ceased to intrigue Dillinger. The natives respectfully made way for them. Otherwise, except for timid glances from the children, they were ignored.

They reached the first huts and paused, looking down the village street. Mouth-watering odors of a feast in preparation reminded Dillinger that he had missed breakfast. At the far end of the street, near the largest hut, native men and women stood quietly in line. Dillinger waited helplessly for some official acknowledgment of his presence.

Suddenly Fornri appeared before him, and accepted his hand. "We are honored," Fornri said, but his face, usually so blandly expressionless, revealed an emotion which Dillinger found difficult to interpret. Was he angry, or merely uneasy? "May I inquire as to the purpose of your visit?" he asked.

Dillinger looked at Protz, who shrugged and looked the other way. "I came to . . . to observe," Dillinger said lamely.

"In the past, you have not interfered in the lives of my people. Is that to be changed?"

"No. I am not here to interfere."

"Then your presence is not required here. This does not concern you."

"Everything that happens on Langri concerns me," Dillinger said. "I came to learn what is happening here. I intend to know."

Fornri withdrew abruptly. Dillinger watched him walk away, watched a group of young natives gather around him. Their manner was quiet, but urgent.

"Funny thing," Protz mused. "With any primitive society I've ever seen, the old men run things. Here on Langri, it's the young men. I'll bet there isn't a man in that crowd who's much over thirty."

Fornri returned. He was uneasy—there could be no doubt of that. He gazed earnestly at Dillinger's face before he spoke. "We know that you have been a friend to my people, and helped us when you could. It is the Mr. Wembling who is our enemy. If he knew, he would attempt to interfere."

"Mr. Wembling will not interfere," Dillinger said.

"Very well. We are holding an election."

Dillinger felt Protz's hand tighten on his arm. He repeated dumbly, "An election?"

Fornri spoke proudly. "We are electing delegates to a constitutional convention."

An idyllic setting. The forest clearing overlooking the sea. Women preparing a feast. Citizens waiting quietly for their turns in the grass voting hut. Democracy in action.

"When the constitution is approved," Fornri went on, "we shall elect a government. Then we shall apply for membership in the Galactic Federation of Independent Worlds."

"Is it legal?" Protz demanded.

"It is legal," Fornri said. "Our attorney has advised us. The main requirement is fifty per cent literacy. We have over ninety per cent literacy. We could have done it much sooner, you see, but we did not know that we needed only fifty per cent."

"You are to be congratulated," Dillinger said. "If your application for Federation membership is accepted, I suppose your government will force Wembling to leave Langri."

"We intend that Langri shall belong to us. It is the Plan."

Dillinger held out his hand. "I wish you every good fortune with your election, and with your application for Federation membership."

With a last glance at the line by the voting hut, they turned and walked slowly back to the plane. Protz whistled, and rubbed his hands together. "And that," he said, "will finish Wembling."

"At least we've solved the mystery of that unknown ship," Dillinger said. "It was their attorney, coming to advise them and help them draw up a constitution. As for this finishing Wembling, you're wrong. The Wemblings in this galaxy don't finish that easily. He's ready for this. You might almost say he's been expecting it."

"What can he do?"

"No court of justice would make him give up what he already has. The natives can keep him from grabbing more land, but what he's developed will be his. He acquired it in good faith, under a charter granted by the Federation. Maybe he'll get to connect up his sites and own a hundred mile stretch of coast. If he doesn't, he has enough space at each site to build a thundering big resort. These enormous golf courses he's been laying out—that land is developed.

He'll get to keep it, and there'll be room there for another hundred hotels on each site if he wants to build them. He'll flood the sea with pleasure fishermen, and starve the natives."

Dillinger looked back at the village, and shook his head sadly. "Do you realize what a tremendous accomplishment that is? Ninety per cent literacy. How they must have worked! And they were beaten before they started. The poor devils."

V

The normal behavior of a forest trail, Dillinger thought, *would be to wander—around trees, away from thickets, generally following the path of least resistance. This trail did not wander. It might have been laid out by a surveyor, so straight did it run. It was an old trail, and a well-worn trail. Trees must have been cut down, but there were no traces of the stumps.*

Ahead of him, Fornri and a half dozen other young natives kept a steady, killing pace and did not look back. They had covered a good five miles, and there seemed to be no end to it. Dillinger was perspiring, and already tired.

Fornri had come to him at Hotel Langri. "We would like for you to come with us," he said. "You alone." And Dillinger had come.

Hotel Langri was all but deserted. At dawn tomorrow the 984th Squadron would head back into space, where it belonged. Wembling and his workmen had already left. Langri had been returned to the possession of its rightful owners.

It had been an absurdly simply thing, this Plan of the

natives—absurdly simple and devastatingly effective. First there had been the application for Federation membership, which fortunately had arrived in Galaxia just as Dillinger's anonymous letters went off with a resounding explosion that overturned the government, caused a turmoil in the Colonial Bureau and Navy Department, and stirred up repercussions as far away as Langri, where a committee touched down briefly for a stormy investigation.

The application was acted upon immediately, and it received unanimous approval.

Wembling was undisturbed. His attorneys were on the job before the last vote was counted, and the native government received a court order to honor Wembling with firm title to the land he had already developed. This the Langri government did, and so complacently that Wembling slyly added several hundred acres to his claim without stirring up a ripple of protest.

Then came the masterstroke, which not even Wembling had foreseen.

Taxes.

Dillinger had been present when Fornri handed Wembling his first tax billing from the government of Langri. Wembling had screamed himself hoarse, and pounded his desk, and vowed he would fight it through every court in the galaxy, but he found the courts to be strangely out of sympathy with him.

If the elected representatives of the people of Langri wished to impose an annual property tax equal to ten times the property's assessed valuation, that was their legal right. It was Wembling's misfortune that he owned the only property on the planet which had an assessed valuation worth recording. Ten times the worth of a grass hut was a negligible value above zero. Ten times the worth of Wembling's hotels amounted to ruin.

The judges were in perfect agreement with Wembling that the government's action was unwise. It would discourage construction and industry and hold back the planet's development indefinitely. In time that would be perfectly obvious to the people of Langri, and then it would be their privilege to elect representatives who would write more lenient tax laws.

In the meantime, Wembling must pay the tax.

It left him a choice of not paying and being ruined, or paying and being much more severely ruined, and he chose not to pay. The government confiscated his property for nonpayment of taxes, and the Langri situation was resolved to the satisfaction of all but Wembling and his backers. Hotel Langri was to become a school and university for the native children. The offices of government would occupy one of the other hotels. The natives were undecided as to what to do with the third, but Dillinger was certain they would use it wisely.

As for Wembling, he was now an employee of the people of Langri. Even the natives admired the way he got things done, and there were islands, many islands, it turned out, far out in the sea where happy vacationers would not interfere with the natives' fishing grounds. Would Mr. Wembling, Fornri asked, like to build hotels on those islands and run them for the Government of Langri? Mr. Wembling would. Mr. Wembling did, in fact, wonder why he had not thought of that in the first place. He negotiated a contract with the natives' attorney, moved his men to the islands, and enthusiastically began planning a whole series of hotels.

Dillinger, following the natives along a forest path, felt

serenely at peace with himself and the galaxy around him.

The path ended in an enormous clearing, carpeted with thick grass and flowers. Dillinger stopped to look around, saw nothing, and hurried to catch the natives.

On the opposite side of the clearing was another path, but this one ended abruptly at a rough pile of stones, a cairn, perhaps, jutting up from the forest floor. Beyond it, rusting, overgrown with vines, hidden by towering trees, lay an old survey ship.

"One of your people once came to live among us," Fornri said. "This was his ship."

The natives stood with hands clasped behind them, their heads bowed reverently. Dillinger waited, wondering what was expected of him. Finally he asked, "There was just one man?"

"Just one," Fornri said. "We have often thought that there may be those who wondered what happened to him. Perhaps you could tell them."

"Perhaps I could," Dillinger said. "I'll see."

He struggled through the undergrowth and circled the ship, looking for a name or an identification number. There was none. The air lock was closed. As Dillinger stood contemplating it, Fornri said, "You may enter if you like. We have placed his things there."

Dillinger walked up the wobbly ramp, and stumbled along a dark passageway. The dim light that filtered into the control room gave the objects there a ghostlike aspect. On a table by the control panel were small mementos, personal effects, books, piles of papers. Dillinger thoughtfully handled a rusted pocket knife, a rosary, a broken compass.

The first book he picked up was a diary. George F.

O'Brien's diary. The entries, written in a precisely penciled hand, were too dim to read. He took the books and papers to the air lock, sat down on the ramp, and began to turn the pages.

There were detailed entries describing O'Brien's early days on the planet, more than a century before. Then the entries became less regular, the dates uncertain as O'Brien lost track of time. Dillinger came to the end, found a second volume, and continued reading.

Just another freebooter, he thought, kicking around on a strange planet, prospecting for metals, enjoying himself with a native harem. Surely it was not this man . . .

The change came subtly down through the years, as O'Brien came to identify himself with the natives, became one of them, and finally faced the future. There was an astute summary of Langri's potential as a resort planet, that might have been written by Wembling. There was a dire warning as to the probable fate of the natives. "If I live," O'Brien had written, "I do not think this will happen."

And if he should not live?

"Then the natives must be taught what to do. There must be a Plan. These things the natives must know."

Government and language. Interplanetary relations. History. Economics, commerce and money. Politics. Law and colonial procedure. Science.

"Not just one man!" Dillinger exclaimed to himself. "He couldn't have!"

The initial landing, probably by a survey ship. Steps to observe in capturing the crew. Negotiations, list of violations and penalties. Achievement of independent status. Steps to Federation membership. Steps to follow when independent status was violated.

"Not just one man!"

It was all there, laboriously written out by an uneducated man who had vision and wisdom and patience. By a great man. It was a brilliant prognostication, with nothing lacking but Wembling's name—and Dillinger had the impression that O'Brien had known more than a few Wemblings in his day. It was all there, everything that had happened, right up to the final master stroke, the ten-to-one tax rate on the hotels.

Dillinger closed the last notebook, carried the papers back to the control room and carefully rearranged things as he had found them. Some day Langri would have its own historians, who would sift through these papers and send the name of George F. O'Brien across the galaxy in dryly-written tomes read only by other historians. The man deserved a better fate.

But perhaps verbal tradition would keep his memory a living thing on Langri far into the future. Perhaps, even now, around the fires, there were legendary tales of what O'Brien had done and said. Or perhaps not. It was difficult for an outsider to probe into such matters, especially if he were a naval officer. That sort of thing required a specialist.

Dillinger took a last look at the humble relics, took a step backwards, and came to a full salute.

He left the ship, carefully closing the air lock behind him. Dusk had settled quickly there, deep in the forest, but the natives were waiting, still in attitudes of reverence.

"I suppose you've looked those things over," Dillinger said.

Fornri seemed startled. "No . . ."

"I see. Well, I found out—as much as there is to find out

about him. If he has any family surviving, I'll see that they know what happened to him."

"Thank you," Fornri said.

"Were there no others who came and lived among you?"

"He was the only one."

Dillinger nodded. "O'Brien was a truly great man. I wonder if you fully realize that. I suppose in time you'll have O'Brien villages and O'Brien streets and O'Brien buildings, and all that sort of thing, but he deserves a really important monument. Perhaps—a planet can be named after a man, you know. You should have named your planet O'Brien."

"O'Brien?" Fornri said. He looked blankly at the others, turned back to Dillinger. "O'Brien? Who is O'Brien?"

THE PLAGUE

By Teddy Keller

Sergeant Major Andrew McCloud ignored the jangling telephones and the excited jabber of a room full of brass, and lit a cigarette. Somebody had to keep his head in this mess. Everybody was about to flip.

Like the telephone. Two days ago Corporal Bettijean Baker had been answering the rare call on the single line—in that friendly, husky voice that gave even generals pause—by saying, "Good morning. Office of the Civil Health and Germ Warfare Protection Co-ordinator." Now there was a switchboard out in the hall with a web of lines running to a dozen girls at a half dozen desks wedged into the outer office. And now the harried girls answered with a hasty, "Germ War Protection."

All the brass hats in Washington had suddenly discovered this office deep in the recesses of the Pentagon. And none of them could quite comprehend what had happened. The situation might have been funny, or at least pathetic, if it hadn't been so desperate. Even so, Andy McCloud's nerves and patience had frayed thin.

"I told you, general," he snapped to the flustered brigadier, "Colonel Patterson was retired ten days ago. I don't know what happened. Maybe this replacement sawbones got strangled in red tape. Anyhow, the brand-new lieutenant hasn't showed up here. As far as I know, I'm in charge."

"But this is incredible," a two-star general wailed. "A mysterious epidemic is sweeping the country, possibly an insidious germ attack timed to precede an all-out invasion, and a noncom is sitting on top of the whole powder keg."

Andy's big hands clenched into fists and he had to wait a moment before he could speak safely. Doggone the freckles and the unruly mop of hair that give him such a boyish look. "May I remind you, general," he said, "that I've been entombed here for two years. My staff and I know what to do. If you'll give us some co-operation and a priority, we'll try to figure this thing out."

"But good heavens," a chicken colonel moaned, "this is all so irregular. A noncom!" He said it like a dirty word.

"Irregular, hell," the brigadier snorted, the message getting through. "There're ways. Gentlemen, I suggest we clear out of here and let the sergeant get to work." He took a step toward the door, and the other officers, protesting and complaining, moved along after him. As they drifted out, he turned and said, "We'll clear your office for top priority." Then dead serious, he added, "Son, a whole nation could panic at any moment. You've got to come through."

Andy didn't waste time standing. He merely nodded to the general, snubbed out his cigarette and buzzed the intercom. "Bettijean, will you bring me all the latest reports, please?" Then he peeled out of his be-ribboned blouse and rolled up his sleeves. He allowed himself one moment to enjoy the sight of the slim, black-headed corporal who entered his office.

Bettijean crossed briskly to his desk. She gave him a

motherly smile as she put down a thick sheaf of papers. "You look beat," she said. "Brass give you much trouble?"

"Not much. We're top priority now." He ran fingers through the thick, brown hair and massaged his scalp, trying to generate stimulation to his weary and confused brain. "What's new?"

"I've gone through some of these," she said. "Tried to save you a little time."

"Thanks. Sit down."

She pulled up a chair and thumbed through the papers. "So far, no fatalities. That's why there's no panic yet, I guess. But it's spreading like . . . well, like a plague." Fear flickered deep in her dark eyes.

"Any water reports?" Andy asked.

"Wichita O.K., Indianapolis O.K., Tulsa O.K., Buffalo O.K.—and a bunch more. No indication there. Except"—she fished out a one-page report—"some little town in Tennessee. Yesterday there was a campaign for everybody to write their congressman about some deal and today they were to vote on a new water system. Hardly anybody showed up at the polls. They've all got it."

Andy shrugged. "You can drink the water, but don't vote for it. Oh, that's a big help." He rummaged through the clutter on his desk and came up with a crude chart. "Any trends yet?"

"It's hitting everybody," Bettijean said helplessly. "Not many kids so far, thank heavens. But housewives, businessmen, office workers, teachers, preachers—rich, poor—from Florida to Alaska. Just when you called me in, one of the girls thought she had a trend. The isolated mountain areas of the West and South. But reports are too fragmentary."

"What is it?" he cried suddenly, banging the desk. "People deathly ill, but nobody dying. And doctors can't identify the poison until they have a fatality for an autopsy. People stricken in every part of the country, but the water systems are pure. How does it spread?"

"In food?"

"How? There must be hundreds of canneries and dairies and packing plants over the country. How could they all goof at the same time—even if it was sabotage?"

"On the wind?"

"But who could accurately predict every wind over the entire country—even Alaska and Hawaii—without hitting Canada or Mexico? And why wouldn't everybody get it in a given area?"

Bettijean's smooth brow furrowed and she reached across the desk to grip his icy, sweating hands. "Andy, do . . . do you think it's . . . well, an enemy?"

"I don't know," he said. "I just don't know."

For a long moment he sat there, trying to draw strength from her, punishing his brain for the glimmer of an idea. Finally, shaking his head, he pushed back into his chair and reached for the sheaf of papers.

"We've got to find a clue—a trend—an inkling of something." He nodded toward the outer office. "Stop all incoming calls. Get those girls on lines to hospitals in every city and town in the country. Have them contact individual doctors in rural areas. Then line up another relief crew, and get somebody carting in more coffee and sandwiches. And on those calls, be sure we learn the sex, age and occupation of the victims. You and I'll start with Washington."

Bettijean snapped to her feet, grinned her encouragement and strode from the room. Andy could hear her crisp instructions to the girls on the phones. Sucking air through his teeth, he reached for his phone and directory.

He dialed until every finger of his right hand was sore. He spoke to worried doctors and frantic hospital administrators and hysterical nurses. His firm, fine penmanship deteriorated to a barely legible scrawl as writer's cramp knotted his hand and arm. His voice burned down to a rasping whisper. But columns climbed up his rough chart and broken lines pointed vaguely to trends.

It was hours later when Bettijean came back into the office with another stack of papers. Andy hung up his phone and reached for a cigarette. At that moment the door banged open. Nerves raw, Bettijean cried out. Andy's cigarette tumbled from trembling fingers.

"Sergeant," the chicken colonel barked, parading into the office.

Andy swore under his breath and eyed the two young officers who trailed after the colonel. Emotionally exhausted, he had to clamp his jaw against a huge laugh that struggled up in his throat. For just an instant there, the colonel had reminded him of a movie version of General Rommel strutting up and down before his tanks. But it wasn't a swagger stick the colonel had tucked under his arm. It was a folded newspaper. Opening it, the colonel flung it down on Andy's desk.

"RED PLAGUE SWEEPS NATION," the scare headline screamed. Andy's first glance caught such phrases as "alleged Russian plot" and "germ warfare" and "authorities hopelessly baffled."

Snatching the paper, Andy balled it and hurled it from him. "That'll help a lot," he growled hoarsely.

"Well, then, sergeant." The colonel tried to relax his square face, but tension rode every weathered wrinkle and fear glinted behind the pale gray eyes. "So you finally recognize the gravity of the situation."

Andy's head snapped up, heated words searing toward his lips. Bettijean stepped quickly around the desk and laid a steady hand on his shoulder.

"Colonel," she said levelly, "you should know better than that."

A shocked young captain exploded, "Corporal. Maybe you'd better report to—"

"All right," Andy said sharply. For a long moment he stared at his clenched fists. Then he exhaled slowly and, to the colonel, flatly and without apology, he said, "You'll have to excuse the people in this office if they overlook some of the G.I. niceties. We've been without sleep for two days, we're surviving on sandwiches and coffee, and we're fighting a war here that makes every other one look like a Sunday school picnic." He felt Bettijean's hand tighten reassuringly on his shoulder and he gave her a tired smile. Then he hunched forward and picked up a report. "So say what you came here to say and let us get back to work."

"Sergeant," the captain said, as if reading from a manual, "insubordination cannot be tolerated, even under emergency conditions. Your conduct here will be noted and—"

"Oh, good heavens!" Bettijean cried, her fingers biting into Andy's shoulder. "Do you have to come in here trying to throw your weight around when this man—"

"That's enough," the colonel snapped. "I had hoped that you two would co-operate, but . . ." He let the sentence trail off as he swelled up a bit with his own importance. "I have turned Washington upside down to get these two officers from the surgeon general's office. Sergeant. Corporal. You are relieved of your duties as of this moment. You will report to my office at once for suitable disciplinary action."

Bettijean sucked in a strained breath and her hand flew to her mouth. "But you can't—"

"Let's go," Andy said, pushing up from his chair. Ignoring the brass, he turned to her and brushed his lips across hers. "Let them sweat a while. Let 'em have the whole stinking business. Whatever they do to us, at least we can get some sleep."

"But you can't quit now," Bettijean protested. "These brass hats don't know from—"

"Corporal!" the colonel roared.

And from the door, an icy voice said, "Yes, colonel?"

The colonel and his captains wheeled, stared and saluted. "Oh, general," the colonel said. "I was just—"

"I know," the brigadier said, stepping into the room. "I've been listening to you. And I thought I suggested that everybody leave the sergeant and his staff alone."

"But, general, I—"

The general showed the colonel his back and motioned Andy into his chair. He glanced to Bettijean and a smile warmed his wedge face. "Corporal, were you speaking just then as a woman or as a soldier?"

Crimson erupted into Bettijean's face and her tight laugh said many things. She shrugged. "Both I guesss."

The general waved her to a chair and, oblivious of the colonel, pulled up a chair for himself. The last trace of humor drained from his face as he leaned elbows on the desk. "Andy, this is even worse than we had feared."

Andy fumbled for a cigarette and Bettijean passed him

a match. A captain opened his mouth to speak, but the colonel shushed him.

"I've just come from Intelligence," the general said. "We haven't had a report—nothing from our agents, from the Diplomatic Corps, from the civilian newspapermen—not a word from any Iron Curtain country for a day and a half. Everybody's frantic. The last item we had—it was a coded message the Reds tried to censor—was an indication of something big in the works."

"A day and a half ago," Andy mused. "Just about the time we knew we had an epidemic. And about the time they knew it."

"It could be just propaganda," Bettijean said hopefully, "proving that they could cripple us from within."

The general nodded. "Or it could be the softening up for an all-out effort. Every American base in the world is alerted and every serviceman is being issued live ammunition. If we're wrong, we've still got an epidemic and panic that could touch it off. If we're right . . . well, we've got to know. What can you do?"

Andy dropped his haggard face into his hands. His voice came through muffled. "I can sit here and cry." For an eternity he sat there, futility piling on helplessness, aware of Bettijean's hand on his arm. He heard the colonel try to speak and sensed the general's movement that silenced him.

Suddenly he sat upright and slapped a palm down on the desk. "We'll find your answers, sir. All we ask is co-operation."

The general gave both Andy and Bettijean a long, sober look, then launched himself from the chair. Pivoting, he said, "Colonel, you and your captains will be stationed by that switchboard out there. For the duration of this emergency, you will take orders only from the sergeant and the corporal here."

"But, general," the colonel wailed, "a noncom? I'm assigned—"

The general snorted. "Insubordination cannot be tolerated—unless you find a two-star general to outrank me. Now, as I said before, let's get out of here and let these people work."

The brass exited wordlessly. Bettijean sighed noisily. Andy found his cigarette dead and lit another. He fancied a tiny lever in his brain and he shifted gears to direct his thinking back into the proper channel. Abruptly his fatigue began to lift. He picked up the new pile of reports Bettijean had brought in.

She moved around the desk and sat, noting the phone book he had used, studying the names he had crossed off. "Did you learn anything?" she asked.

Andy coughed, trying to clear his raw throat. "It's crazy," he said. "From the Senate and House on down, I haven't found a single government worker sick."

"I found a few," she said. "Over in a Virginia hospital."

"But I did find," Andy said, flipping through pages of his own scrawl, "a society matron and her social secretary, a whole flock of office workers—business, not government— and new parents and newly engaged girls and . . ." He shrugged.

"Did you notice anything significant about those office workers?"

Andy nodded. "I was going to ask you the same, since I was just guessing. I hadn't had time to check it out."

"Well, I checked some. Practically none of my victims

came from big offices, either business or industry. They were all out of one- and two-girl offices or small businesses."

"That was my guess. And do you know that I didn't find a doctor, dentist or attorney?"

"Nor a single postal worker."

Andy tried to smile. "One thing we do know. It's not a communicable thing. Thank heaven for—"

He broke off as a cute blonde entered and put stacks of reports before both Andy and Bettijean. The girl hesitated, fidgeting, fingers to her teeth. Then, without speaking, she hurried out.

Andy stared at the top sheet and groaned. "This may be something. Half the adult population of Aspen, Colorado, is down."

"What?" Bettijean frowned over the report in her hands. "It's the same thing—only not quite as severe—in Taos and Santa Fe, New Mexico."

"Writers?"

"Mostly. Some artists, too, and musicians. And poets are among the hard hit."

"This is insane," Andy muttered. "Doctors and dentists are fine—writers and poets are sick. Make sense out of that."

Bettijean held up a paper and managed a confused smile. "Here's a country doctor in Tennessee. He doesn't even know what it's all about. Nobody's sick in his valley."

"Somebody in our outer office is organized," Andy said, pulling at his cigarette. "Here're reports from a dozen military installations all lumped together."

"What does it show?"

"Black-out. By order of somebody higher up—no medical releases. Must mean they've got it." He scratched the growing stubble on his chin. "If this were a fifth column setup, wouldn't the armed forces be the first hit?"

"Sure." Bettijean brightened, then sobered. "Maybe not. The brass could keep it secret if an epidemic hit an army camp. And they could slap a control condition on any military area. But the panic will come from the general public."

"Here's another batch," Andy said. "Small college towns under twenty-five thousand population. All hard hit."

"Well, it's not split intellectually. Small colleges and small offices and writers get it. Doctors don't and dentists don't. But we can't tell who's got it on the military bases."

"And it's not geographical. Look, remember those two reports from Tennessee? That place where they voted on water bonds or something, everybody had it. But the country doctor in another section hadn't even heard of it." Andy could only shake his head.

Bettijean heaved herself up from the chair and trudged back to the outer office. She returned momentarily with a tray of food. Putting a paper cup of coffee and a sandwich in front of Andy, she sat down and nibbled at her snack like an exhausted chipmunk.

Andy banged a fist at his desk again. Coffee splashed over the rim of his cup onto the clutter of papers. "It's here," he said angrily. "It's here somewhere, but we can't find it."

"The answer?"

"Of course. What is it that girls in small offices do or eat or drink or wear that girls in large offices don't do or eat or drink or wear? What do writers and doctors do differently? Or poets and dentists? What are we missing? What—"

In the outer office a girl cried out. A body thumped

against a desk, then a chair, then to the floor. Two girls screamed.

Andy bolted up from his chair. Racing to the door, he shouted back to Bettijean, "Get a staff doctor and a chemist from the lab."

It was the girl who had been so nervous in his office earlier. Now she lay in a pathetic little heap between her desk and chair, whimpering, shivering, eyes wide with horror. The other girls clustered at the hall door, plainly ready to stampede.

"It's not contagious," Andy growled. "Find some blankets or coats to cover her. And get a glass of water."

The other girls, glad for the excuse, dashed away. Andy scooped up the fallen girl and put her down gently on the close-jammed desks. He used a chair cushion for a pillow. By then the other girls were back with a blanket and the glass of water. He covered the girl, gave her a sip of water and heard somebody murmur, "Poor Janis."

"Now," Andy said brightly, "how's that, Janis?"

She mustered a smile, and breathed, "Better. I . . . I was so scared. Fever and dizzy . . . symptoms like the epidemic."

"Now you know there's nothing to be afraid of," Andy said, feeling suddenly and ridiculously like a pill roller with a practiced bedside manner. "You know you may feel pretty miserable, but nobody's conked out with this stuff yet."

Janis breathed out and her taut body relaxed.

"Don't hurry," Andy said, "but I want you to tell me everything that you did—everything you ate or drank—in the last . . . oh, twelve hours." He felt a pressure behind him and swiveled his head to see Bettijean standing there. He tried to smile.

reports. He was still poring over them when the general arrived. Half a dozen other brass hats, none of whom had been to bed, were close behind. The lab technician arrived a minute later. He shook his head as he handed his hastily scribbled report to Andy.

It was Bettijean who squeezed into the office and broke the brittle silence. "Andy, for heaven's sake, what is it?" Then she moved around the desk to stand behind him as he faced the officers.

"Have you got something?" the brigadier asked. "Some girl outside was babbling about writers and doctors, and dentists and college students, and little secretaries and big secretaries. Have you established a trend?"

Andy glanced at the lab report and his smile was as relieved as it was weary. "Our problem," he said, "was in figuring out what a writer does that a doctor doesn't—why girls from small offices were sick—and why senators and postal workers weren't—why college students caught the bug and people in a Tennessee community didn't.

"The lab report isn't complete. They haven't had time to isolate the poison and prescribe medication. But"—he held up a four-cent stamp—"here's the villain, gentlemen."

The big brass stood stunned and shocked. Mouths flapped open and eyes bugged at Andy, at the stamp.

Bettijean said, "Sure. College kids and engaged girls and new parents and especially writers and artists and poets— they'd all lick lots of stamps. Professional men have secretaries. Big offices have postage-meter machines. And government offices have free franking. And"—she threw her arms around the sergeant's neck—"Andy, you're wonderful."

"The old American ingenuity," the colonel said, reaching

for Andy's phone. "I knew we could lick it. Now all we
have to do—"

"At ease, colonel," the brigadier said sharply. He waited
until the colonel had retreated, then addressed Andy. "It's
your show. What do you suggest?"

"Get somebody—maybe even the President—on all radio
and TV networks. Explain frankly about the four-centers
and warn against licking *any* stamps. Then—"

He broke off as his phone rang. Answering, he listened
for a moment, then hung up and said, "But before the big
announcement, get somebody checking on the security clear-
ances at whatever plant it is where they print stamps. This
is a big deal. Somebody may've been planted years ago for
this operation. It shouldn't be too hard.

"But there's no evidence it was a plot yet. Could be sure
accident—some chemical in the stickum spoiled. Do they
keep the stickum in barrels? Find out who had access. And
. . . oh, the phone call. That was the lab. The antidote's
simple and the cure should be quick. They can phone or
broadcast the medical information to doctors. The man on
the phone said they could start emptying hospitals in six
hours. And maybe we should release some propaganda.
'United States whips mystery virus,' or something like that.
And we could send the Kremlin a stamp collection and . . .
Aw, you take it, sir. I'm pooped."

The general wheeled to fire a salvo of commands. Officers
poured into the corridor. Only the brigadier remained, a
puzzled frown crinkling his granite brow.

"But you said that postal workers weren't getting sick."

Andy chuckled. "That's right. Did you ever see a post
office clerk lick a stamp? They always use a sponge."

The general looked to Bettijean, to Andy, to the stamp. He grinned and the grin became a rumbling laugh. "How would you two like a thirty-day furlough to rest up—or to get better acquainted?"

Bettijean squealed. Andy reached for her hand.

"And while you're gone," the general continued, "I'll see what strings I can pull. If I can't wangle you a couple of battlefield commissions, I'll zip you both through O.C.S. so fast you won't even have time to pin on the bars."

But neither Andy nor Bettijean had heard a word after the mention of furlough. Like a pair of puppylovers, they were sinking into the depths of each other's eyes.

And the general was still chuckling as he picked up the lone four-cent stamp in his left hand, made a gun of his right hand, and marched the stamp out of the office under guard.

REMEMBER
THE ALAMO!

By T. R. Fehrenbach

Toward sundown, in the murky drizzle, the man who called himself Ord brought Lieutenant Colonel William Barrett Travis word that the Mexican light cavalry had completely invaded Bexar, and that some light guns were being set up across the San Antonio River. Even as he spoke, there was a flash and bang from the west, and a shell screamed over the old mission walls. Travis looked worried.

"What kind of guns?" he asked.

"Nothing to worry about, sir," Ord said. "Only a few one-pounders, nothing of respectable siege caliber. General Santa Anna has had to move too fast for any big stuff to keep up." Ord spoke in his odd accent. After all, he was a Britainer, or some other kind of foreigner. But he spoke good Spanish, and he seemed to know everything. In the four or five days since he had appeared he had become very useful to Travis.

Frowning, Travis asked, "How many Mexicans, do you think, Ord?"

"Not more than a thousand, now," the dark-haired, blue-eyed young man said confidently. "But when the main body arrives, there'll be four, five thousand."

Travis shook his head. "How do you get all this informa-

tion, Ord? You recite it like you had read it all some place
—like it were history."

Ord merely smiled. "Oh, I don't know *everything,* colonel.
That is why I had to come here. There is so much we don't
know about what happened . . . I mean, sir, what will
happen—in the Alamo." His sharp eyes grew puzzled for an
instant. "And some things don't seem to match up, somehow—"

Travis looked at him sympathetically. Ord talked queerly
at times, and Travis suspected he was a bit deranged. This
was understandable, for the man was undoubtedly a Britainer aristocrat, a refugee from Napoleon's thousand-year
Empire. Travis had heard about the detention camps and
the charcoal ovens . . . but once, when he had mentioned
the *Empereur's* sack of London in '06, Ord had gotten a
very queer look in his eyes, as if he had forgotten completely.

But John Ord, or whatever his name was, seemed to be
the only man in the Texas forces who understood what
William Barrett Travis was trying to do. Now Travis looked
around at the thick adobe wall surrounding the old mission
in which they stood. In the cold, yellowish twilight even
the flaring cook fires of his hundred and eighty-two men
could not dispel the ghostly air that clung to the old place.
Travis shivered involuntarily. But the walls were thick, and
they could turn one-pounders. He asked, "What was it you
called this place, Ord . . . the Mexican name?"

"The Alamo, sir." A slow, steady excitement seemed to
burn in the Britainer's bright eyes. "Santa Anna won't forget that name, you can be sure. You'll want to talk to the
other officers now, sir? About the message we drew up for
Sam Houston?"

"Yes, of course," Travis said absently. He watched Ord head for the walls. No doubt about it, Ord understood what William Barrett Travis was trying to do here. So few of the others seemed to care.

Travis was suddenly very glad that John Ord had shown up when he did.

On the walls, Ord found the man he sought, broad-shouldered and tall in a fancy Mexican jacket. "The commandant's compliments, sir, and he desires your presence in the chapel."

The big man put away the knife with which he had been whittling. The switchblade snicked back and disappeared into a side pocket of the jacket, while Ord watched it with fascinated eyes. "What's old Bill got his britches hot about this time?" the big man asked.

"I wouldn't know, sir," Ord said stiffly and moved on.

Bang-bang-bang roared the small Mexican cannon from across the river. *Pow-pow-pow!* The little balls only chipped dust from the thick adobe walls. Ord smiled.

He found the second man he sought, a lean man with a weathered face, leaning against a wall and chewing tobacco. This man wore a long, fringed, leather lounge jacket, and he carried a guitar slung beside his Rock Island rifle. He squinted up at Ord. "I know . . . I know," he muttered. "Willy Travis is in an uproar again. You reckon that colonel's commission the Congress up at Washington-on-the-Brazos give him swelled his head?"

Rather stiffly, Ord said, "Colonel, the commandant desires an officers' conference in the chapel, now." Ord was somewhat annoyed. He had not realized he would find these Americans so—distasteful. Hardly preferable to Mexicans, really. Not at all as he had imagined.

For an instant he wished he had chosen Drake and the Armada instead of this pack of ruffians—but no, he had never been able to stand sea sickness. He couldn't have taken the Channel, not even for five minutes.

And there was no changing now. He had chosen this place and time carefully, at great expense—actually, at great risk, for the X-4-A had aborted twice, and he had had a hard time bringing her in. But it had got him here at last. And, because for a historian he had always been an impetuous and daring man, he grinned now, thinking of the glory that was to come. And he was a participant—much better than a ringside seat! Only he would have to be careful, at the last, to slip away.

John Ord knew very well how this coming battle had ended, back here in 1836.

He marched back to William Barrett Travis, clicked heels smartly. Travis' eyes glowed; he was the only senior officer here who loved military punctilio. "Sir, they are on the way."

"Thank you, Ord." Travis hesitated a moment. "Look, Ord. There will be a battle, as we know. I know so little about you. If something should happen to you, is there anyone to write? Across the water?"

Ord grinned. "No, sir. I'm afraid my ancestor wouldn't understand."

Travis shrugged. Who was he to say that Ord was crazy? In this day and age, any man with vision was looked on as mad. Sometimes, he felt closer to Ord than to the others.

The two officers Ord had summoned entered the chapel. The big man in the Mexican jacket tried to dominate the wood table at which they sat. He towered over the slender, nervous Travis, but the commandant, straight-backed and arrogant, did not give an inch. "Boys, you know Santa Anna has invested us. We've been fired on all day—" He seemed to be listening for something. *Wham!* Outside, a cannon split the dusk with flame and sound as it fired from the walls. "There is my answer!"

The man in the lounge coat shrugged. "What I want to know is what our orders are. What does old Sam say? Sam and me were in Congress once. Sam's got good sense; he can smell the way the wind's blowin'." He stopped speaking and hit his guitar a few licks. He winked across the table at the officer in the Mexican jacket who took out his knife. "Eh, Jim?"

"Right," Jim said. "Sam's a good man, although I don't think he ever met a payroll."

"General Houston's leaving it up to me," Travis told them.

"Well, that's that," Jim said unhappily. "So what you figurin' to do, Bill?"

Travis stood up in the weak, flickering candlelight, one hand on the polished hilt of his saber. The other two men winced, watching him. "Gentlemen, Houston's trying to pull his militia together while he falls back. You know Texas was woefully unprepared for a contest at arms. The general's idea is to draw Santa Anna as far into Texas as he can, then hit him when he's extended, at the right place and right time. But Houston needs more time—Santa Anna's moved faster than any of us anticipated. Unless we can stop the Mexican Army and take a little steam out of them, General Houston's in trouble."

Jim flicked the knife blade in and out. "Go on."

"This is where we come in, gentlemen. Santa Anna can't leave a force of one hundred eighty men in his rear. If we hold fast, he must attack us. But he has no siege equip-

ment, not even large field cannon." Travis' eye gleamed.
"Think of it, boys! He'll have to mount a frontal attack,
against protected American riflemen. Ord, couldn't your
Englishers tell him a few things about that!"

"Whoa, now," Jim barked. "Billy, anybody tell you there's
maybe four or five thousand Mexicaners comin'?"

"Let them come. Less will leave!"

But Jim, sour-faced turned to the other man. "Davey?
You got something to say?"

"Hell, yes. How do we get out, after we done pinned
Santa Anna down? You thought of that, Billy boy?"

Travis shrugged. "There is an element of grave risk, of
course. Ord, where's the document, the message you wrote
up for me? Ah, thank you." Travis cleared his throat.
"Here's what I'm sending on to General Houston." He read,
"Commandancy of the Alamo, February 24, 1836 . . . are
you sure of the date, Ord?"

"Oh, I'm sure of that," Ord said.

"Never mind—if you're wrong we can change it later. 'To
the People of Texas and all Americans in the World. Fellow
Freemen and Compatriots! I am besieged with a thousand or
more Mexicans under Santa Anna. I have sustained a con-
tinual bombardment for many hours but have not lost a
man. The enemy has demanded surrender at discretion,
otherwise, the garrison is to be put to the sword, if taken.
I have answered the demand with a cannon shot, and our
flag still waves proudly over the walls. I shall never surrender or retreat. Then, I call on you in the name of liberty,
of patriotism and everything dear to the American character—,' " He paused, frowning. "This language seems pretty
old-fashioned, Ord—"

"Oh, no, sir. That's exactly right," Ord murmured.

" '. . . To come to our aid with all dispatch. The enemy is receiving reinforcements daily and will no doubt increase to three or four thousand in four or five days. If this call is neglected, I am determined to sustain myself as long as possible and die like a soldier who never forgets what is due his honor or that of his homeland. VICTORY OR DEATH!' "

Travis stopped reading, looked up. "Wonderful! Wonderful!" Ord breathed. "The greatest words of defiance ever written in the English tongue—and so much more literate than that chap at Bastogne."

"You mean to send that?" Jim gasped.

The man called Davey was holding his head in his hands.

"You object, Colonel Bowie?" Travis asked icily.

"Oh, cut that 'colonel' stuff, Bill," Bowie said. "It's only a National Guard title, and I like 'Jim' better, even though I am a pretty important man. Damn right I have an objection! Why, that message is almost aggressive. You'd think we wanted to fight Santa Anna! You want us to be marked down as warmongers? It'll give us trouble when we get to the negotiation table—"

Travis' head turned. "Colonel Crockett?"

"What Jim says goes for me, too. And this: I'd change that part about all Americans, et cetera. You don't want anybody to think we think we're better than the Mexicans. After all, Americans are a minority in the world. Why not make it 'all men who love security'? That'd have worldwide appeal—"

"Oh, Crockett," Travis hissed.

Crockett stood up. "Don't use that tone of voice to me, Billy Travis! That piece of paper you got don't make you

no better'n us. I ran for Congress twice, and won. I know
what the people want—"

"What the people want doesn't mean a damn right now,"
Travis said harshly. "Don't you realize the tyrant is at the
gates?"

Crockett rolled his eyes heavenward. "Never thought I'd
hear a good American say that! Billy, you'll never run for
office—"

Bowie held up a hand, cutting into Crockett's talk. "All
right, Davey. Hold up. You ain't runnin' for Congress now.
Bill, the main thing I don't like in your whole message is
that part about victory or death. That's got to go. Don't ask
us to sell that to the troops!"

Travis closed his eyes briefly. "Boys, listen. We don't have
to tell the men about this. They don't need to know the real
story until it's too late for them to get out. And then we
shall cover ourselves with such glory that none of us shall
ever be forgotten. Americans are the best fighters in the
world when they are trapped. They teach this in the Foot
School back on the Chatahoochee. And if we die, to die
for one's country is sweet—"

"Hell with that," Crockett drawled. "I don't mind dyin',
but not for these big landowners like Jim Bowie here. I just
been thinkin'—I don't own nothing in Texas."

"I resent that," Bowie shouted. "You know very well I
volunteered, after I sent my wife off to Acapulco to be with
her family." With an effort, he calmed himself. "Look,
Travis. I have some reputation as a fighting man—you know
I lived through the gang wars back home. It's obvious this
Alamo place is indefensible, even if we had a thousand
men."

"But we must delay Santa Anna at all costs—"

Bowie took out a fine, dark Mexican cigar and whittled at it with his blade. Then he lit it, saying around it, "All right, let's all calm down. Nothing a group of good men can't settle around a table. Now listen. I got in with this revolution at first because I thought old Emperor Iturbide would listen to reason and lower taxes. But nothin's worked out, because hotheads like you, Travis, queered the deal. All this yammerin' about liberty! Mexico is a Republic, under an Emperor, not some kind of democracy, and we can't change that. Let's talk some sense before it's too late. We're all too old and too smart to be wavin' the flag like it's the Fourth of July. Sooner or later, we're goin' to have to sit down and talk with the Mexicans. And like Davey said, I own a million hectares, and I've always paid minimum wage, and my wife's folks are way up there in the Imperial Government of the Republic of Mexico. That means I got influence in all the votin' groups, includin' the American Immigrant, since I'm a minority group member myself. I think I can talk to Santa Anna, and even to old Iturbide. If we sign a treaty now with Santa Anna, acknowledge the law of the land, I think our lives and property rights will be respected—" He cocked an eye toward Crockett.

"Makes sense, Jim. That's the way we do it in Congress. Compromise, everybody happy. We never allowed ourselves to be led nowhere we didn't want to go, I can tell you! And Bill, you got to admit that we're in better bargaining position if we're out in the open, than if old Santa Anna's got us penned up in this old Alamo."

"Ord," Travis said despairingly. "Ord, you understand. Help me! Make them listen!"

Ord moved into the candlelight, his lean face sweating.

"Gentlemen, this is all wrong! It doesn't happen this way—"

Crockett sneered, "Who asked you, Ord? I'll bet you ain't even got a poll tax!"

Decisively, Bowie said, "We're free men, Travis, and we won't be led around like cattle. How about it, Davey? Think you could handle the rear guard, if we try to move out of here?"

"Hell, yes! Just so we're movin'!"

"O.K. Put it to a vote of the men outside. Do we stay, and maybe get croaked, or do we fall back and conserve our strength until we need it? Take care of it, eh, Davey?"

Crockett picked up his guitar and went outside.

Travis roared, "This is insubordination! Treason!" He drew his saber, but Bowie took it from him and broke it in two. Then the big man pulled his knife.

"Stay back, Ord. The Alamo isn't worth the bones of a Britainer, either."

"Colonel Bowie, please," Ord cried. "You don't understand! You *must* defend the Alamo! This is the turning point in the winning of the west! If Houston is beaten, Texas will never join the Union! There will be no Mexican War. No California, no nation stretching from sea to shining sea! This is the Americans' manifest destiny. You are the hope of the future . . . you will save the world from Hitler, from Bolshevism—"

"Crazy as a hoot owl," Bowie said sadly. "Ord, you and Travis got to look at it both ways. We ain't all in the right in this war—we Americans got our faults, too."

"But you are free men," Ord whispered. "Vulgar, opinionated, brutal, but free! You are still better than the breed who kneels to tyranny—"

Crockett came in. "O.K., Jim."

"How'd it go?"

"Fifty-one per cent for hightailin' it right now."

Bowie smiled. "That's a flat majority. Let's make tracks."

"Comin', Bill?" Crockett asked. "You're O.K., but you just don't know how to be one of the boys. You got to learn that no dog is better'n any other."

"No," Travis croaked hoarsely. "I stay. Stay or go, we shall all die like dogs, anyway. Boys, for the last time! Don't reveal our weakness to the enemy—"

"What weakness? We're stronger than them. Americans could whip the Mexicans any day, if we wanted to. But the thing to do is make 'em talk, not fight. So long, Bill."

The two big men stepped outside. In the night there was a sudden clatter of hoofs as the Texans mounted and rode. From across the river came a brief spatter of musket fire, then silence. In the dark, there had been no difficulty in breaking through the Mexican lines.

Inside the chapel, John Ord's mouth hung slackly. He muttered, "Am I insane? It didn't happen this way—it couldn't! The books can't be *that* wrong—"

In the candlelight, Travis hung his head. "We tried, John. Perhaps it was a forlorn hope at best. Even if we had defeated Santa Anna, or delayed him, I do not think the Indian Nations would have let Houston get help from the United States."

Ord continued his dazed muttering, hardly hearing.

"We need a contiguous frontier with Texas," Travis continued slowly, just above a whisper. "But we Americans have never broken a treaty with the Indians, and pray God we never shall. *We* aren't like the Mexicans, always pushing, always grabbing off New Mexico, Arizona, California. *We* aren't colonial oppressors, thank God! No, it wouldn't have worked out, even if we American immigrants had secured our rights in Texas—" He lifted a short, heavy, percussion pistol in his hand and cocked it. "I hate to say it, but perhaps if we hadn't taken Payne and Jefferson so seriously—if we could only have paid lip service, and done what we really wanted to do, in our hearts . . . no matter. I won't live to see our final disgrace."

He put the pistol to his head and blew out his brains.

Ord was still gibbering when the Mexican cavalry stormed into the old mission, pulling down the flag and seizing him, dragging him before the resplendent little general in green and gold.

Since he was the only prisoner, Santa Anna questioned Ord carefully. When the sharp point of a bayonet had been thrust half an inch into his stomach, the Britainer seemed to come around. When he started speaking, and the Mexicans realized he was English, it went better with him. Ord was obviously mad, it seemed to Santa Anna, but since he spoke English and seemed educated, he could be useful. Santa Anna didn't mind the raving; he understood all about Napoleon's detention camps and what they had done to Britainers over there. In fact, Santa Anna was thinking of setting up a couple of those camps himself. When they had milked Ord dry, they threw him on a horse and took him along.

Thus John Ord had an excellent view of the battlefield when Santa Anna's cannon broke the American lines south of the Trinity. Unable to get his men across to safety, Sam Houston died leading the last, desperate charge against the Mexican regulars. After that, the American survivors were too tired to run from the cavalry that pinned them against the flooding river. Most of them died there. Santa Anna expressed complete indifference to what happened to the Texans' women and children.

Mexican soldiers found Jim Bowie hiding in a hut, wearing a plain linen tunic and pretending to be a civilian. They would not have discovered his identity had not some of the Texan women whom the cavalry had captured cried out, "Colonel Bowie—Colonel Bowie!" as he was led into the Mexican camp.

He was hauled before Santa Anna, and Ord was summoned to watch. "Well, Don Jaime," Santa Anna remarked, "You have been a foolish man. I promised your wife's uncle to send you to Acapulco safely, though of course your lands are forfeit. You understand we must have lands for the veterans' program when this campaign is over—" Santa Anna smiled then. "Besides, since Ord here has told me how instrumental you were in the abandonment of the Alamo, I think the Emperor will agree to mercy in your case. You know, Don Jaime, your compatriots had me worried back there. The Alamo might have been a tough nut to crack . . . *pues,* no matter."

And since Santa Anna had always been broadminded, not objecting to light skin or immigrant background, he invited Bowie to dinner that night.

Santa Anna turned to Ord. "But if we could catch this rascally war criminal, Crockett . . . however, I fear he has escaped us. He slipped over the river with a fake passport, and the Indians have interned him."

"Si, *Señor Presidente,*" Ord said dully.

"Please, don't call me that," Santa Anna cried, looking around. "True, many of us officers have political ambitions, but Emperor Iturbide is old and vain. It could mean my head—"

Suddenly, Ord's head was erect, and the old, clear light was in his blue eyes. "Now I understand!" he shouted. "I thought Travis was raving back there, before he shot himself —and your talk of the Emperor! American respect for Indian rights! Jeffersonian form of government! Oh, those ponces who peddled me that X-4-A—the *track jumper!* I'm not back in my own past. I've jumped the time track—*I'm back in a screaming alternate!*"

"Please not so loud, *Señor* Ord." Santa Anna sighed. "Now, we must shoot a few more American officers, of course. I regret this, you understand, and I shall no doubt be much criticized in French Canada and Russia, where there are still civilized values. But we must establish the Republic of the Empire once and for all upon this continent, that aristocratic tyranny shall not perish from the earth. Of course, as an Englishman, you understand perfectly, Señor Ord."

"Of course, excellency," Ord said.

"There are soft hearts—soft heads, I say—in Mexico who cry for civil rights for the Americans. But I must make sure that Mexican dominance is never again threatened north of the Rio Grande."

"*Seguro,* excellency," Ord said, suddenly. If the bloody X-4-A *had* jumped the track, there, was no getting back, none at all. He was stuck here. Ord's blue eyes narrowed. "After all, it . . . it is manifest destiny that the Latin peoples of North America meet at the center of the continent. Canada and Mexico shall share the Mississippi."

Santa Anna's dark eyes glowed. "You say what I have often thought. You are a man of vision, and much sense.

You realize the *Indios* must go, whether they were here first or not. I think I will make you my secretary, with the rank of captain."

"*Gracias,* Excellency."

"Now, let us write my communique to the capital, *Capitán* Ord. We must describe how the American abandonment of the Alamo allowed me to press the traitor Houston so closely he had no chance to maneuver his men into the trap he sought. *Ay, Capitán,* it is a cardinal principle of the Anglo-Saxons, to get themselves into a trap from which they must fight their way out. This I never let them do, which is why I succeed where others fail . . . you said something, *Capitán?*"

"*Sí,* Excellency. I said, I shall title our communique: 'Remember the Alamo,'" Ord said, standing at attention.

"*Bueno!* You have a gift for words. Indeed, if ever we feel the *gringos* are too much for us, your words shall once again remind us of the truth!" Santa Anna smiled. "I think I shall make you a major. You have indeed coined a phrase which shall live in history forever!"

THE HUNCH

By Christopher Anvil

Stellar Scout James Connely and Sector Chief of Scouts Gregory MacIntyre eyed each other with mutual suspicion. Connely, his blood pressure already well above normal, could see that this latest meeting was going to develop along the lines of those that had gone before.

"Look, Mac," said Connely, "my ship's fine. I'm fine. I don't need anything re-equipped. Spare me the new improvements and just let me know—What's the job this time?"

MacIntyre, a powerfully-built man with heavy brows and light-blue eyes of unusual brilliance, watched Connely with that look of alert concentration seen on bullfighters, duellists, and cats springing for mice.

"This isn't the usual scout job," said MacIntyre emphatically. "We've sent out two ships four months apart, and heard nothing more from either. Obviously they came up against something that outclassed them."

MacIntyre gestured at the new and weird devices that sat on tables and chairs around the room. "We flatly will not let you go out half-equipped. This job is risky."

Connely looked at the new equipment with no enthusiasm, and jerked a thumb in the direction of his ship, "Look, I can already outfight any ordinary ship up to twice the weight of my own. I keep away from territory infested with commerce raiders. If I do get surprised, my ship's as fast as they come. If I have to, I can even outrun the Space Force."

MacIntyre snorted. "The Space Force. Who cares about them? When they aren't hide-bound, they're budget-bound. I hate to hear an Interstellar Scout measure himself by the Space Force."

"Mac," said Connely, lowering his voice with an effort, "it took me six months to figure out that last batch of new equipment you put in the ship. Some of that stuff is fine, and some of it's poison. Now that I know which is which, *leave it alone.*"

MacIntyre visibly controlled himself. "Why don't we at least try to be logical about this, Con?"

"Sure. Go ahead."

"All right. Now, look. These two ships I've mentioned went out on the same route you're going to take. They weren't heard from again. They had more advanced equipment than your ship has. *And yet they were lost.*"

"So, you think I should have the same equipment they had, eh?"

"Oh, no, Con." MacIntyre looked shocked. "That's the whole point. We've got *better* equipment, now, and you've got to have it."

"Where were these two ships headed?"

MacIntyre snapped on a three-dimensional stellar projection and pointed out a distant sun-system.

Connely scowled. "The shortest route there is thick with Maury's commerce raiders. That's the worst gang there is. Maury's got a reconverted dreadnought."

"I know," said MacIntyre. He touched a button, and a

complex set of lines appeared in the projection, showing a series of awkward roundabout jumps to detour the dangerous territory.

Connely scowled at the long route. "Damn and blast commerce raiders."

MacIntyre nodded, "With the Space Force tied up in that sector, they crop up like toadstools. But there they are and we have to face it." He snapped a switch, and the projection faded out. "You noticed how complex the detour was? That makes it extra hard to know where the trouble happened. But at least it is obvious that it happened *en route*. As soon as either of those scouts reached his destination, he'd have orbited a signal satellite. The satellite has an automatic trip that triggers a subspace emergency call if it's not canceled every twelve hours. No call has been received. Now, we have no knowledge of anything *natural* along these routes that would finish off two ships four months apart. Therefore, we're up against something man-made."

"An undeclared commerce raider preying on the secondary routes?"

"Most likely," said MacIntyre. "You see how we arrive at this conclusion by simple logic. But let's go further. If the other two ships were lost because of inferior speed or weapons, what we have to do to prevent *your* loss is to remove the inferiority. Therefore, your ship needs to be re-equipped. Q. E. D."

Connely opened his mouth and shut it.

MacIntyre beamed. "All right, Con?" He reached for the work-order.

"No," said Connely. He struggled for an explanation of his own viewpoint and finally said, "The thing doesn't feel right to me, Mac. I've got a hunch the equipment caused the trouble."

MacIntyre's face changed expression several times. As if tasting the sentence, he growled, "I've got a *hunch.*" He nodded his head in disgust and got up. "Well, Con, don't say I didn't warn you." He started for the door, and paused with his hand on the knob. "If you want your mail, incidentally, it's in the top drawer on the left." When he went out, he slammed the door so hard that a badly-balanced piece of equipment slid off a chair, gave a low whistling sound, and lit up in green lights.

Connely blew his breath out and glanced around suspiciously. It was not like MacIntyre to give up without a knock-down, drag-out fight. Puzzled, Connely crossed to MacIntyre's desk and reached down to pull open the drawer.

The faint sound from the device that had slid off the chair rose to a howl the instant Connely touched the drawer handle. The lights on the device all flashed yellow. A thing like a miniature gun popped out of a turret, and gave a high-pitched whistle with a weird variation that riveted Connely's attention. Then bubbles seemed to be bursting in the air all around him. He was conscious of a faint sweetish odor, and of a sensation that he was falling in a long, long, seemingly endless fall.

Connely opened his eyes, to see before him the control board of his ship. Glancing around, he saw a number of changes. On a bulkhead to his left, the meteor-warning gong had been ripped out, and a new panel installed. The panel was covered with toggle switches and pink, green, and flashing yellow lights. Hanging from one of the switches near the bottom of the panel was a note:

Con:

Sorry you got into a disagreement with one of our new items of equipment. But that's life.

As you'll notice, I've re-equipped your ship from end to end. You've even been outfitted with our new reflex helmet and clothing. The instructions for everything but the clothing are attached to the pieces of equipment they refer to. Knowing your violent temper, I've decided to put the instructions for the clothing where you won't be likely to tear them up in an outburst of rage. Check the other equipment, and you'll find the instructions for your garments, too.

You'll notice that your course has been all taped and set up in the new-type course control. Keep your eyes open, make the best use of your new equipment, and perhaps you'll succeed where the men before you failed.

As for your mail—you couldn't read it while you were here, and you'd be distracted if you read it out there—so I will hold it against your return.

                                  All the best,
                                       Mac

Connely stared at the note, then nodded sourly. Mac had done it again. Now it would be Connely's job to stay alive in a ship crammed with new equipment just one jump out of the experimental stage. Connely bent, raised an edge of his non-regulation gray carpet, and dropped the note underneath for future reference. He scowled at the new panel with its colored lights, and saw a slim brown envelope hanging beside the cabinet, and marked, "Instructions."

Connely took down the envelope, glanced over several sheets of instructions and diagrams, and found that the panel was a supplementary control box for various new devices installed all over the ship—such of them as were not purely automatic. From this panel, Connely worked his way slowly toward the rear of the ship. He found numerous changes. The already strong frame had been reinforced by heavy cross-members that angled through the ship, half-blocking the corridors. Everything metal had a peculiar gloss that refused to dent under the roughest treatment Connely dared to give it.

A variety of new weapons had been installed, including one whose thick instruction manual asserted that it fired "holes." Each piece of equipment had its own weighty instruction manual, and the combined mass of information presented in these manuals made Connely feel dizzy.

After he'd glanced through an unusually complicated manual, Connely paused to scratch his head. He immediately felt as if someone had placed a hand on top of his head and given a sharp twist. There was a low *whir,* his vision cut off, and something gave his hand a painful whack.

Then something spun across his face, and Connely's vision returned.

Cautiously, he raised his hand and felt the slick glossy surface of some kind of helmet. As long as he felt along the surface of the helmet, nothing happened. As soon as he tried to touch his face, however, the helmet spun around, giving his head a sharp twist in the process, and knocked his hand out of the way. This, Connely realized, must be the "reflex helmet" MacIntyre had mentioned in his note. Connely tried to get hold of the edge of the helmet to take it off, but whenever his hand approached the edge, the helmet swiveled rapidly, to knock his hand away.

This, Connely conceded, might be a very fine defense if

someone was trying to smash his face in with a club. But how did he get out of the thing, anyway?

A few minutes of neck-wrenching experiments convinced him that the quickest way would be to locate the instructions. But he had by now worked his way back almost to the drive unit, and he had seen nothing of any instructions so far. He pulled open the door of the drive chamber, looked inside, and swallowed hard. The old drive was gone, and in its place sat a monstrous unit of such dimensions that special handholds had been installed to make it possible to climb back around it. Gradually it dawned on Connely that the new drive unit took up so much space that it actually projected forward into the place formerly occupied by the fuel tanks. In order to fit the drive unit in, the fuel tanks had been ripped out. Connely blinked, and glanced all around. *Where was the fuel?*

He climbed into the drive chamber, looked around, climbed up and around past a number of blocky projections, and eventually located a container not much bigger than a foot-locker, that was surrounded by big coils and a complicated arrangement of braces, wires, and tubes. This was such a formidable-looking thing that Connely was careful not to even touch it. He crouched in the narrow space between the tank—if that was what it was—and a projecting bulge on the drive unit. He reached carefully in without touching the maze of wires and tubes and got the instruction manual dangling behind it. Sure enough, the manual was labeled, "Fuel Tank M81-x, Service and Operating Instructions."

Scowling, Connely flipped back past diagrams and data tables, and was relieved to find a summary at the end. He skimmed it rapidly, then slowed as he came to a section that read:

". . . the tank, therefore, 'contains' only the head end of each keyed chain of packed fuel molecules. The remainder of each chain is selectively distorted into subspace. This allows for a very great reduction in the size of the fuel tank. It is, however, MOST IMPORTANT that no interruption in the action of the subspace-control unit be permitted to take place. Should such interruption occur, the normal volume of the molecules, no longer distorted into subspace, will attempt to fill the tank. The tank, of course, cannot possibly contain this volume of fuel. It will, therefore, burst. The outsurge of fuel, no longer molecularly oriented, and removed from contact with the negative catalyst layers of tank and fuel lines, will explode. As no part of the ship can possibly survive the release of such quantities of energy, it is strongly recommended that the preventive maintenance procedures in this manual be thoroughly understood BEFORE the tank is filled."

Connely swallowed, shut the manual, and started to get up. The back of his head bumped the bulge on the drive unit. He slouched a little to avoid banging into the drive unit again, and as he did so he came close to one of a number of copper-colored tubes that angled up from the tank to the drive unit. There was a whir, a twist at the top of his head, and his vision cut off. Alarmed, he tried to ease himself back to a sitting position. There was another sharp twist, as the helmet spun around again. He had a momentary glimpse of blurred light, then *Bang!*—the edge of the helmet hit the drive unit and knocked his head forward. Immediately there was another whir and another twist. *Whack! Bang!*

Bathed in sweat, Connely dropped to a sitting position on the metal deck, and sat as motionless as he could. The helmet came to a stop. He drew in a shaking breath and looked around. Everything seemed to be all right. He edged carefully out from under the bulge of the drive unit and got to his feet, still clutching the instruction manual. Gradually he relaxed, and began to breathe easily again. He grabbed a nearby handhold to climb back into the forward part of the ship, and cast a last glance back at the fuel tank.

A glittering drop of liquid fell from a bend in the coppery fuel line, hit the top of tank, and disappeared.

Connely, frozen into a state of paralysis, watched the dripping fuel for some time. With unvarying regularity, each drop appeared at the same point on the tube, fell in the same way through a maze of wires and supports, and hit the top of the tank, to vanish without a trace. A new drop then formed, to fall in exactly the same way.

Gradually, Connely dragged his gaze from the sight of these falling, highly-explosive drops. He forced himself to move up along the handholds, and gradually worked his way into the front end of the ship. He felt no safer here, but at least, he could move without the fear of doing yet more damage.

He sank into the control seat, pulled out his handkerchief, and reached up to wipe the perspiration out of his eyes.

Whir! His head twisted and his vision cut off. The helmet knocked his hand aside.

Connely sprang to his feet, furious.

The helmet swung around again, and now he could see.

Boiling mad, Connely thumbed through the fuel tank

manual, hoping against hope that the instruction sheet for the helmet was inside somewhere. But it wasn't there.

Connely pulled back his rug, got out MacIntyre's note, and read: ". . . Knowing your violent temper, I've decided to put the instructions for the clothing where you won't be likely to tear them up . . . Check the other equipment, and you'll find the instructions for your garments—"

Connely read this over several times and swore savagely. He *had* checked the other pieces of equipment! Angrily, he shoved the note back under the rug, and straightened up. A flashing yellow light on the new panel caught his eye.

Having skimmed through the sheet of instructions for that panel, Connely knew that a flashing yellow light indicated something that needed attention. The light for the fuel tank was still glowing a comfortable green and he had checked everything else, so what was that one flashing light for?

Connely asked himself if he could possibly have missed some piece of equipment? If so, maybe MacIntyre had put the instructions for the helmet near that very piece of equipment. Connely got out the list that identified the various lights, checked it through carefully, and discovered something called "IntruGrab M1-X, Medium."

What in space, Connely asked himself, is an "IntruGrab?" He stared at the diagram, found the location of the thing, and trod down the corridor, pausing here and there to duck under or climb over the reinforcing structural members that got in his way. When he came to the spot marked on the diagram, the only thing there was the inner space-lock door. Connely glanced around, and turned to go back to the control room.

From somewhere came a faint thumping sound. He stopped, and tried without success to locate it. He stepped back around a beam and looked up. Over his head was a hemisphere of metal plate and shiny metal bars wrapped around a transparent globe.

Inside the globe, red-faced, furious, and hammering on the transparent surface with a calloused fist, was Sector Chief of Scouts Gregory MacIntyre.

At first, Connely couldn't believe it. He climbed up on a beam for a closer look, and MacIntyre glared out at him through the transparent layer. When Connely merely stared, MacIntyre jabbed a finger at something out of Connely's range of vision, opened his mouth as if shouting, shook his fist at Connely, drew a finger across his throat and then banged his fist against the transparent layer, which gave forth a faint thump.

Connely shrugged and reached up for the instruction manual which was tied by a string to one of the bars. Once he had the manual, he dropped off the beam and walked back up the corridor, a smile on his face. He was aware that at any moment the ship might still be exploded into its component atoms. Or a commerce raider might appear from nowhere and reel him in on a souped-up gravitor beam. But for some reason these thoughts no longer bothered him. He settled down comfortably in the control room and flipped through the instruction manual for the Model M1-X Intru-Grab (medium). Connely hoped to find the instructions for his helmet—but they weren't there. Scowling, he went back to the beginning of the manual, and carefully worked his way past diagrams and descriptions, noting a sentence here and a technical detail there, which gave him enough to go on so that he saw the purpose and general mode of operation of the device even before he read the final paragraph at the back of the manual:

"In brief, the M1-X IntruGrab (medium) is designed to prevent human or other intruders from gaining entrance to restricted localities. Once keyed to the physical characteristics of the personnel legitimately present, and activated to prevent entry of others, the IntruGrab will selectively remove unauthorized intruders, will imprison such intruders for an indefinite period, removing waste products and providing minimal nutritive requirements according to the specifications table on page 32. The IntruGrab (medium) will handle individuals from the size of a grasshopper to that of an adult male gorilla, and will signal capture by flashlight light, tone alarm, or other standard warning mechanism. *CAUTION:* The manufacturers do not warrant use of the M1-X IntruGrab (medium) for any purpose contrary to local statute or ordinance. *Consult your lawyer or local law-enforcement agencies before installing.*"

Connely skimmed back through the manual to the instructions for releasing captured intruders. He discovered that there were two methods of release: permanent, and provisional. He decided he should not over-burden his mind by studying too much at once, so he only learned how to release an intruder provisionally. Armed with this information, he went back down the corridor, and looked up.

MacIntyre was glaring down through the bars with a look that would have shriveled the self-confidence of almost any subordinate. Connely, however, had not gravitated into the Stellar Scouts by accident, and so as he looked back at MacIntyre, a grin gradually spread over his face. This brought MacIntyre to a state of boiling rage bordering on apoplexy.

Connely, alarmed lest MacIntyre hurt himself, mentally reviewed the instructions, then raised his hand toward the globe. An orange light blinked on.

"Lower," said Connely.

The globe came down on a frame like a set of lazy tongs. A number of plastic tubes snapped loose from the globe and coiled up into the ceiling.

"Release," said Connely.

The transparent layer slid back, the bars came open, and MacIntyre stumbled out. The cage went back up to the ceiling, and MacIntyre swayed unsteadily on his feet.

It occurred to Connely that the food served by the M1-X IntruGrab (medium) was probably pretty poor stuff, to say nothing of being locked up in the thing for all this time. He guided MacIntyre down the corridor to the control room, helped him sit down, and got some instant-heated hot broth for him.

"Thanks," said MacIntyre, his voice hardly more than a croak. He glared across the room at the new control panel, then looked away. He stiffened his jaw and said nothing.

Connely cheerfully refrained from making any comment. He thought the situation was sufficiently clear as it was. While he was enjoying a sensation of comfortable superiority, the aroma of the hot broth made him aware that he was extremely hungry. He got some of the same broth for himself, and raised a steaming spoonful.

Whir. The helmet whipped around, knocked the spoon out of his hand, and splashed most of the hot broth from the spoon across his face. When he tried to wipe off his face, the helmet knocked his hand away.

Connely, boiling mad, but unwilling to admit the fix he

was in, said casually, "By the way, Mac, where are the instructions for this helmet?"

"In the Mangle," said MacIntyre, his voice hoarse.

Connely frowned. He had no memory of any "Mangle." He checked the list of devices controlled from the new panel and found no "Mangle" listed. Mentally, he worked his way from the front of the ship to the rear, crossing off the places he had already looked over. Suddenly he realized that he hadn't looked in the General Supplies storeroom.

Connely went back along the corridor, opened an airtight door, went down a short cross-corridor, and opened the door to his left. Inside, cramping the shelves and bins of parts and equipment, stood an enigmatic gray block about six feet wide, eight feet high, and twelve feet long, with smoothly rounded corners. Connely touched it, and it gave him a snappy shock. Connely looked all around it. A single lens, about an inch across, and set about eighteen inches below the top, traveled around from side to side as if keeping an eye on him.

Connely lost patience, and muttered to himself, "Where in space is the manual for this thing?"

A wide slot promptly popped open in the side nearest him. A gray oblong about an inch thick by eight inches wide popped out, and folded apart down the center to reveal a gray metal book marked with glossy black lettering: "Mangle MI-X (small, medium, large) Instruction Manual."

Connely flipped back the flexible metal pages of this book, which were almost hot to the touch. Between the last page and the back cover was a sheet of what appeared to be fine charcoal. Connely looked at it closely, and an odor of creosote and wood alcohol wafted up to meet him. It dawned on

Connely that this must be the remains of the instruction sheet he wanted.

Connely went back to the control room, and found MacIntyre looking much improved. Connely, using short and simple language, described the trouble he'd had with the Mangle, the new fuel tank, and the "reflex helmet."

MacIntyre looked serious. "That business with the fuel tank sounds bad."

"Oh," said Connely, "the *fuel tank* sounds bad, does it? I have to eat, you know. How do I get out of this helmet?"

MacIntyre appeared to be searching his memory. He said hesitantly. "To tell you the truth, Con, the microcircuit for that helmet was so unusual, and I got so interested in it, that I don't believe I ever *did* read the operating instructions."

Connely restrained himself with an effort. In a very low voice, he said, "You don't happen to have any suggestions, do you, Mac?"

"Hm-m-m," said MacIntyre. "Well, maybe we could *squirt* the food in?"

This suggestion left Connely speechless. Before he had recovered, the annunciator gave a buzz, and announced in its synthetic voice: "Ship sighted. Class III cruiser, identity unknown. No recognition signal."

MacIntyre growled, "A Space Force ship would have identified itself right away. That must be the raider we're looking for."

Connely whirled to thrust the drive control full ahead. The accelerometer needle wound around its dial in a tribute to the power of the ship's monster drive unit. The communications screen cut into the battle-control circuit to show a small green image being overaken by a much larger red image.

After a little while, Connely saw that the cruiser was losing its struggle to narrow the gap fast enough, and stepped over to look at the trip meter.

On the rectangular chartlike face above the meter itself a little white dot representing the scout ship was moving past within easy distance of Space Center 7.

MacIntyre said, "As I remember, the fleet based at Seven has half-a-dozen dreadnoughts, and around eighty other ships above the size of scouts. To operate here, any raider would need to be out of his head."

Connely tried the communicator, and could contact neither the cruiser nor Space Center 7.

The annunciator sounded its buzzer. "Ship sighted. Dreadnought of unknown class and identity. No recognition signal."

The battle screen now showed a huge red image closing in fast on an intersecting course. The likelihood of its being on this course by pure chance wasn't worth thinking about.

Connely said, "We're trapped, Mac. We built up so much momentum getting away from that cruiser that we'll land right in the lap of the dreadnought."

"That's the dreadnought's worry," snapped MacIntyre. "With the stuff we've got on board, we could take on the sector fleet."

"If it works."

"It'll work," said MacIntyre positively.

The communicator chimed and Connely snapped it on. A bored voice said, "You come through Maury's territory, you either pay your tariff or we squash you. We already picked off two of you little bugs."

Connely snapped off the communicator and glanced at MacIntyre.

MacIntyre said, "We can't be in Maury's territory. I specifically set up the course to avoid that."

Connely snapped on the communicator. "According to our trip-meter, we're nowhere near Maury's territory."

"Your trip-meter must have a busted bolt, pal. Now cut out the 6-V act and pay your tariff like a good little boy. Or get squashed."

MacIntyre knocked forward a lever that put the handling of the ship and its weapons completely under control of the battle computer.

On the viewscreen a pair of the dreadnought's monster turrets lit up in a white blaze as the fusion guns let loose their warning blasts. The scout ship continued on its course.

MacIntyre set his jaw. Connely, bathed in sweat, watched the two screens.

On the battle screen, a burst of yellow lines left the dreadnought as ultrafast missiles and missile-killers streaked out on their tracks. The dreadnought lit with dazzling blasts from its fusion weapons, and the space-distorters of the two ships reflected these blasts, to hurl the searing bolts of energy back and forth between them. Enormous blue-white blurs reached out from the dreadnought, to haul the scout ship bodily off its course.

Connely felt a gathering vibration of the deck underfoot. On the screen, the racing missiles arced in, like a fist closing to squash a gnat. Then the overloaded space-distorters ceased to throw the fusion bolts back at the dreadnought, but merely deflected them into space.

The yellow tracks of the missiles abruptly ended. It took

Connely a few seconds to realize that the space-distorters, in deflecting the accumulated fusion blasts from the dreadnought, had done it with such accuracy as to burn up every missile approaching the scout ship. A small faint dotted line traveled from the scout ship to the huge red image of the dreadnought. Red dots began appearing here and there all over the battle screen.

Connely blinked and glanced at the outside viewscreen. The dreadnought, filling the screen from end to end, was fast taking on the look of a piece of Swiss cheese. As Connely watched, chunks of armor plate and turret vanished right and left, leaving round holes several yards across.

A thin purple fan now reached out on the battle screen from the scout ship to the dreadnought. On the outside viewscreen, the dreadnought appeared to lengthen out like an image on a sheet of live rubber. It stretched out into an elongated cylinder dotted with oval slits. Abruptly the fan faded. The cylinder snapped back, and the viewscreen showed the dreadnought with the look of a ground car that has just run into a tree at a hundred and fifty miles an hour.

Connely and MacIntyre looked at each other. MacIntyre grinned suddenly, "Well, Con, *now* what do you have to say about new equipment? Without the new drive the cruiser would have gotten us. Without the new weapons, the dreadnought would have."

"It's not *new* equipment I'm against," said Connely, "but unreliable equipment. And I never saw a piece of new equipment yet that didn't have at least one nasty shock built into it."

"The new drive and weapons saved us."

"And the leak the new helmet put in the new fuel line may finish us."

"Oh," said MacIntyre. "I forgot that." He grabbed the fuel tank instruction manual, and instantly buried himself in it.

Connely hit the Astroposit button, and a few moments later, a piece of paper tape unrolled, giving position based on a comparison of the stellar patterns around them with known stellar patterns. This informed them that they were right in the middle of Maury's territory.

Scowling, Connely glanced at the trip-meter, which showed distance traveled so far, and, in its projected chart showed the ship drawing away from Space Center 7. Connely looked at the trip-meter, a standard item of equipment, as if it were a traitor. He pulled off inspection covers, peered in with lights and jointed mirrors, and found nothing wrong. Next he looked suspiciously at the new course-control, where MacIntyre had set up his course. A look into this strange item merely confused Connely, so he contented himself with a study of the instruction manual.

After a considerable time, MacIntyre handed Connely the tank instruction manual, and pointed out a paragraph:

"Node Effect. *CAUTION!* Do not touch exterior surface of fuel tank while subspace control unit is in operation. Such contact may unbalance the matter-energy equilibrium designed into the tank, causing momentary formation of a subspace node at the point of contact. That portion of an object within the node will be projected into subspace and may not reappear within several light-years of the tank. Severe injury may result."

"Evidently," said MacIntyre, "the dripping fuel is being thrown harmlessly into subspace. Since there's a special repair kit for the fuel line, I think we can fix it all right."

Connely sighed in relief. "Good. Now let me show you

something." He handed MacIntyre a big sheet of thin paper thick with diagrams and text in fine type, that had been pasted into an envelope in the back of the course-control manual.

MacIntyre scowled at the paper, then squinted at a sentence Connely pointed out, and read aloud:

"Unlike most course-controls, the late model Z60 is perfectly fool proof; if the inexperienced pilot sets the Z60 for an unnecessarily complex route from point to point, the new corrector circuits shorten the route automatically."

MacIntyre looked up, speechless.

"Isn't that nice?" said Connely. "You or I or anyone else painstakingly sets the Z60 for a roundabout route to keep out of dangerous territory. The Z60 then charitably decides we are too ignorant to know there's a shorter way, so it puts us right through the middle of the place where we don't want to go. Meanwhile, the standard trip-meter has no way to know the Z60 has changed the course, so the pilot finds it out when it's too late."

MacIntyre shook his head in disgust.

Connely said, "I had a hunch it was the equipment that was making the trouble. But I didn't have all the facts, so I couldn't *prove* I was right."

"But how," MacIntyre objected, "could you guess what was wrong without knowing the facts? That's not logical."

"It sure isn't. Logic has to do with chains of individual facts. Intuition takes whole groups of facts at once. You can recognize a familiar pattern—like a familiar face—even though you *don't* consciously know all the details. Sometimes it's a mistake, but then you can often use logic as a check. With intuition you see it; with logic you check it."

Connely, now that the excitement was over, was again feeling hungry and uncomfortable. "You don't have *any* idea how this helmet works?"

"I think it's a psionic circuit. That's all I can tell you." MacIntyre glared at the course-control manual and suddenly slammed it down. "The devil with it. I'd better fix that fuel line."

As MacIntyre went out, Connely had a vague hunch that something was wrong. However, he was too busy trying to get out of the helmet. Psionics, he told himself, had to do with the interaction of devices and the human organism itself. Maybe mental attitude would affect the helmet. Connely tilted his head forward, and visualized, pleaded, urged, insisted, *believed* that the helmet would fall off.

With a thud the helmet fell to the deck.

For an instant Connely felt as if all his troubles and difficulties were over. Then he saw the familiar flashing yellow light on the new control panel.

The light told him that, like all the other purely machine-like devices on board, the M1-X IntruGrab (medium) was doing its duty with ironclad, black-and-white, absolutely indisputable logic.

But Connely did not belabor the point as, for the second time, he let MacIntyre loose.

BARNACLE BULL

By Winston P. Sanders

The *Hellik Olav* was well past Mars, acceleration ended, free-falling into the Asteroid Belt on a long elliptical orbit, when the interior radiation count began to rise. It wasn't serious, and worried none of the four men aboard. They had been so worried all along that a little extra ionization didn't seem to matter.

But as the days passed, the Geigers got still more noisy. And then the radio quit.

This was bad! No more tapes were being made of signals received—Earth to one of the artificial satellites to Phobos to a cone of space which a rather smug-looking computer insisted held the *Hellik Olav*—for later study by electronics engineers. As for the men, they were suddenly bereft of their favorite programs. Adam Langnes, captain, no longer got the beeps whose distortions gave him an idea of exterior conditions and whose Doppler frequency gave him a check on his velocity. Torvald Winge, astronomer, had no answers to his requests for data omitted from his handbook and computations too elaborate for the ship's digital. Per Helledahl, physicist, heard no more sentimental folk songs nor the recorded babblings of his youngest child. And Erik Bull, engineer, couldn't get the cowboy music sent from the

American radio satellite. He couldn't even get the Russians' Progressive jazz.

Furthermore, and still more ominous, the ship's transmitter also stopped working.

Helledahl turned from its disassembled guts. Despite all he could do with racks, bags, magnetic boards, he was surrounded by a zero gravity halo of wires, resistances, transistors, and other small objects. His moon face peered through it with an unwonted grimness. "I can find nothing wrong," he said. "The trouble must be outside, in the boom."

Captain Langnes, tall and gaunt and stiff of manner, adjusted his monocle. "I dare say we can repair the trouble," he said. "Can't be too serious, can it?"

"It can like the devil, if the radar goes out too," snapped Helledahl.

"Oh, heavens!" exclaimed Winge. His mild, middle-aged features registered dismay. "If I can't maintain my meteorite count, what am I out here for?"

"If we can't detect the big meteorites in time for the autopilot to jerk us off a collision course, you won't be out here very long," said Bull. "None of us will, except as scrap metal and frozen hamburger."

Helledahl winced. "Must you, Erik?"

"Your attitude is undesirable, Herr Bull," Captain Langnes chided. "Never forget, gentlemen, the four of us, crowded into one small vessel for possibly two years, under extremely hazardous conditions, can only survive by maintaining order, self-respect, morale."

"How can I forget?" muttered Bull. "You repeat it every thirty-seven hours and fourteen minutes by the clock." But he didn't mutter very loudly.

"You had best have a look outside, Herr Bull," went on the captain.

"I was afraid it'd come to that," said the engineer dismally. "Hang on, boys, here we go again."

Putting on space armor is a tedious job at best, requiring much assistance. In a cramped air-lock chamber—for lack of another place—and under free fall, it gets so exasperating that one forgets any element of emergency. By the time he was through the outer valve, Bull had invented three new verbal obscenities, the best of which took four minutes to enunciate.

He was a big, blocky, redhaired and freckle-faced young man, who hadn't wanted to come on this expedition. It was just a miserable series of accidents, he thought. As a boy, standing at a grisly hour on a cliff above the Sognefjord to watch the first Sputnik rise, he had decided to be a spaceship engineer. As a youth, he got a scholarship to the Massachusetts Institute of Technology, and afterward worked for two years on American interplanetary projects. Returning home, he found himself one of the few Norwegians with that kind of experience. But he also found himself thoroughly tired of it. The cramped quarters, tight discipline, reconstituted food and reconstituted air and reconstituted conversation, were bad enough. The innumerable petty nuisances of weightlessness, especially the hours a day spent doing ridiculous exercises lest his very bones atrophy, were worse. The exclusively male companionship was still worse: especially when that all-female Russian satellite station generally called the Nunnery passed within view.

"In short," Erik Bull told his friends, "if I want to take

vows of poverty, chastity, and obedience, I'd do better to
sign up as a Benedictine monk. I'd at least have something
drinkable on hand."

Not that he regretted the time spent, once it was safely
behind him. With judicious embroidering, he had a lifetime
supply of dinner-table reminiscences. More important, he
could take his pick of Earthside jobs. Such as the marine
reclamation station his countrymen were building off Sval-
bard, with regular airbus service to Trondheim and Oslo.
There was a post!

Instead of which, he was now spinning off beyond Mars,
hell for leather into a volume of space that had already
swallowed a score of craft without trace.

He emerged on the hull, made sure his life line was fast,
and floated a few minutes to let his eyes adjust. A tiny
heatless sun, too brilliant to look close to, spotted puddles
of undiffused glare among coalsack shadows. The stars, un-
winking, needle bright, were so many that they swamped
the old familiar constellations in their sheer number. He
identified several points as asteroids, some twinkling as
rotation exposed their irregular surfaces, some so close
that their relative motion was visible. His senses did not
react to the radiation, which the ship's magnetic field was
supposed to ward off from the interior but which sharply
limited his stay outside. Bull imagined all those particles
zipping through him, each drilling a neat submicroscopic
hole, and wished he hadn't.

The much-touted majestic silence of space wasn't evident
either. His air pump made too much noise. Also, the suit
stank.

Presently he could make sense out of the view. The ship
was a long cylinder, lumpy where meteor bumpers protected

the most vital spots. A Norwegian flag, painted near the bows, was faded by solar utraviolet, eroded by micrometeoric impacts. The vessel was old, though basically sound. The Russians had given it to Norway for a museum piece, as a propaganda gesture. But then the Americans had hastily given Norway the parts needed to renovate. Bull himself had spent six dreary months helping do that job. He hadn't been too unhappy about it, though. He liked the idea of his country joining in the exploitation of space. Also, he was Americanized enough to feel a certain malicious pleasure when the *Ivan Pavlov* was rechristened in honor of St. Olav.

However, he had not expected to serve aboard the thing!

"O.K., O.K.," he sneered in English, "hold still, Holy Ole, and we'll have a look at your latest disease."

He drew himself back along the line and waddled forward over the hull in stickum boots. Something on the radio transceiver boom . . . what the devil? He bent over. The motion pulled his boots loose. He upended and went drifting off toward Andromeda. Cursing in a lackluster voice, he came back hand over hand. But as he examined the roughened surface he forgot even to be annoyed.

He tried unsuccessfully to pinch himself.

An hour convinced him. He made his laborious way below again. Captain Langnes, who was Navy insisted that you went "below" when you entered the ship, even in free fall. When his spacesuit was off, with only one frost burn suffered from touching the metal, he faced the others across a cluttered main cabin.

"Well?" barked Helledahl. "What is it?"

"As the lady said when she saw an elephant eating cabbages with what she thought was his tail," Bull answered slowly, "if I told you, you wouldn't believe me."

"Of course I would!" said Langnes. "Out with it!"

"Well, skipper . . . we have barnacles."

A certain amount of chemical and biological apparatus had been brought along to study possible effects of the whatever-it-was that seemed to forbid spacecraft crossing the Asteroid Belt. The equipment was most inadequate, and between them the four men had only an elementary knowledge of its use. But then, all equipment was inadequate in zero gravity, and all knowledge was elementary out here.

Work progressed with maddening slowness. And meanwhile the *Hellik Olav* fell outward and outward, on an orbit which would not bend back again until it was three Astronomical Units from the sun. And the ship was out of communication. And the radar, still functional but losing efficiency all the time, registered an ever thicker concentration of meteorites. And the 'tween-decks radiation count mounted, slowly but persistently.

"I vote we go home," said Helledahl. Sweat glistened on his forehead, where he sat in his tiny bunk cubicle without touching the mattress.

"Second the motion," said Bull at once. "Any further discussion? I move the vote. All in favor, say, '*Ja*.' All opposed, shut up."

"This is no time for jokes, Herr Bull," said Captain Langnes.

"I quite agree, sir. And this trip is more than a joke, it's a farce. Let's turn back!"

"Because of an encrustation on the hull?"

Surprisingly, gentle Torvald Winge supported the skipper with almost as sharp a tone. "Nothing serious has yet happened," he said. "We have now shielded the drive tubes so that the barnacle growth can't advance to them. As for our communications apparatus, we have spare parts in ample supply and can easily repair it once we're out of this fantastic zone. Barnacles can be scraped off the radar arms, as well as the vision parts. What kind of cowards will our people take us for, if we give up at the first little difficulty?"

"Live ones," said Helledahl.

"You see," Bull added, "we're not in such bad shape now, but what'll happen if this continues? Just extrapolate the radiation. I did. We'll be dead men on the return orbit."

"You assume the count will rise to a dangerous level," said Winge. "I doubt that. Time enough to turn back, if it seems we have no other hope. But what you don't appreciate, Erik, is the very real, unextrapolated danger of such a course."

"Also, we seem to be on the track of an answer to the mystery—the whole purpose of this expedition," said Langnes. "Given a little more data, we should find out what happened to all the previous ships."

"Including the Chinese?" asked Bull.

Silence descended. They sat in mid-air, reviewing a situation which familiarity did nothing to beautify.

Observations from the Martian moons had indicated the Asteroid Belt was much fuller than astronomers had believed. Of course, it was still a rather hard vacuum . . . but one through which sand, gravel, and boulders went flying with indecent speed and frequency. Unmanned craft were sent in by several nations. Their telemetering instruments confirmed the great density of cosmic debris, which increased as they swung further in toward the central zone. But then they quit sending. They were never heard from again. Manned ships stationed near the computed orbits of the robot vessels, where these emerged from the danger

area, detected objects with radar, panted to match veloc-
ities, and saw nothing but common or garden variety
meteorites.

Finally the Chinese People's Republic sent three craft
with volunteer crews, toward the Belt. One ship went off
course and landed in the Pacific Ocean near San Francisco.
After its personnel explained the unique methods by which
they had been persuaded to volunteer, they were allowed to
stay. The scientists got good technical jobs, the captain
started a restaurant, and the political commissar went on
the lecture circuit.

But the other two ships continued as per instructions.
Their transmission stopped at about the same distance as
the robot radios had, and they were never seen again either.

After that, the big nations decided there was no need
for haste in such expensive undertakings. But Norway had
just outfitted her own spaceship, and all true Norwegians
are crazy. The *Hellik Olav* went out.

Winge stirred. "I believe I can tell you what happened to
the Chinese," he said.

"Sure," said Bull. "They stayed on orbit till it was too
late. Then the radiation got them."

"No. They saw themselves in our own situation, panicked,
and started back."

"So?"

"The meteorites got them."

"Excuse me," said Langnes, obviously meaning it the
other way around. "You know better than that, Professor
Winge. The hazard isn't that great. Even at the highest
possible density of material, the probability of impact with
anything of considerable mass is so low—"

"I am not talking about that, captain," said the astronomer. "Let me repeat the facts *ab initio,* to keep everything systematic, even if you know most of them already.

"Modern opinion holds that the asteroids, and probably most meteorites throughout the Solar System, really are the remnants of a disintegrated world. I am inclined to suspect that a sudden phase change in its core caused the initial explosion—this can happen at a certain planetary mass—and then Jupiter's attraction gradually broke up the larger pieces. Prior to close-range study, it was never believed the asteroidean planet could have been large enough for this to happen. But today we know it must have been roughly as big as Earth. The total mass was not detectable at a distance, prior to space flight, because so much of it consists of small dark particles. These, I believe, were formed when the larger chunks broke up into lesser ones which abraded and shattered each other in collisions, before gravitational forces spread them too widely apart."

"What has this to do with the mess we're in?" asked Bull.

Winge looked startled. "Why . . . that is—" He blushed. "Nothing, I suppose." To cover his embarrassment, he began talking rapidly, repeating the obvious at even greater length:

"We accelerated from Earth, and a long way beyond, thus throwing ourselves into an eccentric path with a semi-major axis of two Astronomical Units. But this is still an ellipse, and as we entered the danger zone, our velocity gained more and more of a component parallel to the planetary orbits. At our aphelion, which will be in the very heart of the Asteroid Belt, we will be moving substantially with the average meteorite. Relative velocity will be very small, or zero. Hence collisions will be rare, and mild when they do occur. Then we'll be pulled back sunward. By the time we start accelerating under power toward Earth, we will again be traveling at a large angle to the natural orbits. But by that time, also, we will be back out of the danger zone.

"Suppose, however, we decided to turn back at this instant. We would first have to decelerate, spending fuel to kill an outward velocity which the sun would otherwise have killed for us. Then we must accelerate inward. We can just barely afford the fuel. There will be little left for maneuvers. *And* . . . we'll be cutting almost perpendicularly across the asteroidal orbits. Their full density and velocity will be directed almost broadside to us.

"Oh, we still needn't worry about being struck by a large object. The probability of that is quite low. But what we will get is the fifteen kilometer-per-second sandblast of the uncountable small particles. I have been computing the results of my investigations so far, and arrive at a figure for the density of this cosmic sand which is, well, simply appalling. Far more than was hitherto suspected. I don't believe our hull can stand such a prolonged scouring, meteor bumpers or no."

"Are you certain?" gulped Helledahl.

"Of course not," said Winge testily. "What is certain, out here? I believe it highly probably, though. And the fact that the Chinese never came back would seem to lend credence to my hypothesis."

The barnacles had advanced astoundingly since Bull last looked at them. Soon the entire ship would be covered, except for a few crucial places toilfully kept clean.

He braced his armored self against the reactive push of

his cutting torch. It was about the only way to get a full-grown barnacle loose. The things melded themselves with the hull. The flame drowned the sardonic stars in his vision but illuminated the growths.

They looked quite a bit like the Terrestrial marine sort. Each humped up in a hard conoidal shell of blackish-brown material. Beneath them was a layer of excreted metal, chiefly ferrous, plated onto the aluminum hull.

I'd hate to try landing through an atmosphere, thought Bull. Of course, that wouldn't be necessary. We would go into orbit around Earth and call for someone to lay alongside and take us off . . . But heading back sunward, we'll have one sweet time controlling internal temperature . . . No, I can simply slap some shiny paint on. That should do the trick. I'd have to paint anyway, to maintain constant radiation characteristics when micrometeorites are forever scratching our metal. Another chore. Space flight is nothing but one long round of chores. The next poet who recites in my presence an ode to man's conquest of the universe can take that universe—every galaxy and every supernova through every last, long light-year—and put . . .

If we get home alive.

He tossed the barnacle into a metal canister for later study. It was still red hot, and doubtless the marvelously intricate organism within the shell had suffered damage. But the details of the lithophagic metabolism could be left for professional biologists to figure out. All they wanted aboard Holy Ole was enough knowledge to base a decision on.

Before taking more specimens, Bull made a circuit of the hull. There were many hummocks on it, barnacles growing upon barnacles. The foresection had turned into a hill of

shells, under which the radio transceiver boom lay buried.
Another could be built when required for Earth approach.
The trouble was, with the interior radiation still mounting—
while a hasty retreat seemed impossible—Bull had started to
doubt he ever would see Earth again.

He scrubbed down the radar, then paused to examine
the spot where he had initially cut off a few dozen samples.
New ones were already burgeoning on the ferroplate left
by their predecessors—little fellows with delicate glasslike
shells which would soon grow and thicken, becoming incredibly tough. Whatever that silicate material was, study
of it should repay Terrestrial industry. Another bonanza
from the Asteroid Belt, the modern Mother Lode.

"Ha!" said Bull.

It had sounded very convincing. The proper way to ex-
ploit space was not to mine the planets, where you must
grub deep in the crust to find a few stingy ore pockets,
then spend fabulous amounts of energy hauling your gains
home. No, the asteroids had all the minerals man would
ever need, in developing his extraterrestrial colonies and on
Earth herself. Freely available minerals, especially on the
metallic asteroids from the core of the ancient planet. Just
land and help yourself. No elaborate apparatus needed to
protect you from your environment. Just the spaceship and
space armor you had to have anyway. No gravitational well
to back down into and climb back out of. Just a simple
thrust of minimum power.

Given free access to the asteroids, even a small nation
like Norway could operate in space, with all the resulting
benefits to her economy, politics, and prestige. And there
was the *Hellik Olav,* newly outfitted, with plenty of volun-

teers—genuine ones—for an exploratory mission and to hell with the danger.

"Ha!" repeated Bull.

He had been quite in favor of the expedition, provided somebody else went. But he was offered a berth and made the mistake of telling his girl.

"Ohhhh, Erik!" she exclaimed, enormous-eyed.

After six months in space helping to rig and test the ship, Bull could have fallen in love with the Sea Hag. However, this had not been necessary. When he had returned to Earth, swearing a mighty oath never to set foot above the stratosphere again, he met Marta. She was small and blond and deliciously shaped. She adored him right back. The only flaw he could find in her was a set of romantic notions about the starry universe and the noble Norwegian destiny therein.

"Oh, oh," he said, recognizing the symptoms. In haste: "Don't get ideas, now. I told you I'm a marine reclamation man, from here on forever."

"But this, darling! This chance! To be one of the conquerors! To make your name immortal!"

"The trouble is, I'm still mortal myself."

"The service you can do—to our country!"

"Uh, apart from everything else, do you realize that, uh, even allowing for acceleration under power for part of the distance, I'd be gone for more than two years?"

"I'll wait for you."

"But—"

"Are you *afraid*, Erik?"

"Well, no. But—"

"Think of the Vikings! Think of Fridtjof Nansen! Think of Roald Amundsen!"

Bull dutifully thought of all these gentlemen. "What about them?" he asked.

But it was a light summer night, and Marta couldn't imagine any true Norwegian refusing such a chance for deathless glory, and one thing sort of led to another. Before he recovered his wits, Bull had accepted the job.

There followed a good deal of work up in orbit, readying the ship, and a shakedown cruise lasting some weeks. When he finally got pre-departure leave, Bull broke every known traffic law and a few yet to be invented, on the way to Marta's home. She informed him tearfully that she was so sorry and she hoped they would always be good friends, but she had been seeing so little of him and had met someone else but she would always follow his future career with the greatest interest. The someone else turned out to be a bespectacled writer who had just completed a three-volume novel about King Harald Hardcounsel (1015–1066). Bull didn't remember the rest of his furlough very clearly.

A shock jarred through him. He bounced from the hull, jerked to a halt at the end of his life line, and waited for the dizziness to subside. The stars leered.

"Hallo! Hallo, Erik! Are you all right?"

Bull shook his head to clear it. Helledahl's voice, phoned across the life line, was tinny in his earphones. "I think so. What happened?"

"A small meteorite hit us, I suppose. It must have had an abnormal orbit to strike so hard. We can't see any damage from inside, though. Will you check the outer hull?"

Bull nodded, though there was no point in doing so.

After he hauled himself back, he needed a while to find the spot of impact. The pebble had collided near the waist of the ship, vaporizing silicate shell material to form a neat little crater in a barnacle hummock. It hadn't quite penetrated to the ferroplate. A fragment remained, trapped between the rough lumps.

Bull shivered. Without that overgrowth, the hull would have been pierced. Not that that mattered greatly in itself. There was enough patching aboard to repair several hundred such holes. But the violence of impact was an object lesson. Torvald Winge was almost certainly right. Trying to cut straight across the Asteroid Belt would be as long a chance as men had ever taken. The incessant bombardment of particles, mostly far smaller than this but all possessing a similar speed, would wear down the entire hull. When it was thin enough to rip apart under stress, no meteor bumpers or patches would avail.

His eyes sought the blue-green glint of Earth, but couldn't find it among so many stars. You know, he told himself, I don't even mind the prospect of dying out here as much as I do the dreariness of it. If we turned around now, and somehow survived, I'd be home by Christmas. I'd only have wasted one extra year in space, instead of more than three—counting in the preparations for this arduous cruise. I'd find me a girl, no, a dozen girls. And a hundred bottles. I'd make up for that year in style, before settling down to do work I really enjoy.

But we aren't likely to survive, if we turn around now.

But how likely is our survival if we keep going—with the radiation shield failing us? And an extra two years on Holy Ole? I'd go nuts!

Judas priest! Was ever a man in such an ugh situation?

Langnes peered at the sheaf of papers in his hand. "I have drafted a report of our findings with regard to the, ah, space barnacles," he said. "I would like you gentlemen to criticize it as I read aloud. We have now accounted for the vanishing of the previous ships—"

Helledahl mopped his brow. Tiny beads of sweat broke loose and glittered in the air. "That doesn't do much good if we also vanish," he pointed out.

"Quite," Langnes looked irritated. "Believe me, I am more than willing to turn home at once. But that is impracticable, as Professor Winge has shown and the unfortunate Chinese example has confirmed."

"I say it's just as impracticable to follow the original orbit," declared Bull.

"I understand you don't like it here," said Winge, "but really, courting an almost certain death in order to escape two more years of boredom seems a trifle extreme."

"The boredom will be all the worse, now that we don't have anything to work toward," said Bull.

The captain's monocle glared at him. "Ahem!" said Langnes. "If you gentlemen are quite through, may I have the floor?"

"Sure," said Bull. "Or the wall or the ceiling, if you prefer. Makes no difference here."

"I'll skip the preamble of the report and start with our conclusions. 'Winge believes the barnacles originated as a possibly mutant life form on the ancient planet before it was destroyed. The slower breakup of the resulting super-asteroidal masses gave this life time to adapt to spatial conditions. The organism itself is not truly protoplasmic. Instead of water, which would either boil or freeze in vacuo at this distance from the sun, the essential liquid is some heavy substance we have not been able to identify except as an aromatic compound.'"

"Aromatic is too polite," said Bull, wrinkling his nose. The air purifiers had still not gotten all the chemical stench out.

Langnes proceeded unrelenting: "'The basic chemistry does remain that of carbon, of proteins, albeit with an extensive use of complex silicon compounds. We theorize the life cycle as follows. The adult form ejects spores which drift freely through space. Doubtless most are lost, but such wastefulness is characteristic of nature on Earth, too. When a spore does chance on a meteorite or an asteroid it can use, it develops rapidly. It requires silicon and carbon, plus traces of other elements; hence it must normally flourish only on stony meteorites, which are, however, the most abundant sort. Since the barnacle's powerful, pseudo-enzymatic digestive processes—deriving their ultimate energy from sunlight—also extract metals where these exist, it must eliminate same, which it does by laying down a plating, molecule by molecule, under its shell. Research into the details of this process should interest both biologists and metallurgists.

"'The shell serves a double function. To some extent, it protects against ionizing radiation of solar or cosmic origin. Also, being a nonconductor, it can hold a biologically generated static charge, which will cause nearby dust to drift down upon it. Though this is a slow method of getting the extra nourishment, the barnacle is exceedingly long-lived, and can adjust its own metabolic and reproductive rates to the exigencies of the situation. Since the charge is not very great, and he himself is encased in metal, a spaceman notices no direct consequences.

" 'One may well ask why this life form has never been observed before. First, it is doubtless confined to the Asteroid Belt, the density of matter being too low elsewhere. We have established that it is poisoned by water and free oxygen, so no spores could survive on any planet man has yet visited, even if they did drift there. Second, if a meteorite covered with such barnacles does strike an atmosphere, the surface vaporization as it falls will destroy all evidence. Third, even if barnacle-crusted meteorites have been seen from spaceships, they look superficially like any other stony objects. No one has captured them for closer examination.' "

He paused to drink water from a squeeze bottle. "Hear, hear," murmured Bull, pretending the captain stood behind a lectern.

"That's why the unmanned probe ships never were found," said Helledahl. "They may well have been seen, more or less on their predicted orbits, but they weren't recognized."

Langnes nodded. "Of course. That comes next in the report. Then I go on to say: 'The reason that radio transmission ceased in the first place is equally obvious. Silicon components are built into the boom, as part of a transistor system. The barnacles ate them.

" 'The observed increase in internal irradiation is due to the plating of heavy metals laid down by the barnacles. First, the static charges and the ferromagnetic atoms interfere with the powerful external magnetic fields which are generated to divert ions from the ship. Second, primary cosmic rays coming through that same plating produce showers of secondary particles.

" 'Some question may be raised as to the explosive growth rate of barnacles on our hull, even after all the silicon available in our external apparatus had been consumed. The answer involves consideration of vectors. The ordinary member of the Asteroid Belt, be it large or small, travels in an orbit roughly parallel to the orbits of all other members. There are close approaches and occasional collisions, but on the whole, the particles are thinly scattered by Terrestrial standards, isolated from each other. Our ship, however, is slanting across those same orbits, thus exposing itself to a veritable rain of bodies, ranging in size from microscopic to sand granular. Even a single spore, coming in contact with our hull, could multiply indefinitely.' "

"That means we're picking up mass all the time," groaned Bull. "Which means we'll accelerate slower and get home even later than I'd feared."

"Do you think we'll get home at all?" fretted Helledahl. "We can expect the interference with our radiation shield, and the accumulation of heavy atoms, to get worse all the time. Nobody will ever be able to cross the Belt!"

"Oh, yes, they will," said Captain Langnes. "Ships must simply be redesigned. The magnetic screens must be differently heterodyned, to compensate. The radio booms must be enclosed in protective material. Or perhaps—"

"I know," said Bull in great weariness. "Perhaps antifouling paint can be developed. Or spaceships can be careened, God help us. Oh, yes. All I care about is how we personally get home. I can't modify our own magnetic generators. I haven't the parts or the tools, even if I knew precisely how. We'll spin on and on, the radiation worse every hour, till—"

"Be quiet!" snapped Langnes.

"The Chinese turned around, and look what happened to them," underlined Winge. "We must try something different, however hopeless it too may look."

Bull braced his heavy shoulders. "See here, Torvald," he growled, "what makes you so sure the Chinese did head back under power?"

"Because they were never seen again. If they had been on the predicted orbit, or even on a completed free-fall ellipse, one of the ships watching for them in the neighborhood of Earth would have— Oh."

"Yes," said Bull through his teeth. "Would have seen them? How do you know they weren't seen? I think they were. I think they plugged blindly on as they'd been ordered to, and the radiation suddenly started increasing on a steep curve—as you'd expect, when a critical point of fouling up was passed. I think they died, and came back like comets, sealed into spaceships so crusted they looked like ordinary meteorites!"

The silence thundered.

"So we may as well turn back," said Bull at last. "If we don't make it, our death'll be a quicker and cleaner one than those poor devils had."

Again the quietude. Until Captain Langnes shook his head. "No. I'm sorry, gentlemen. But we go on."

"What?" screamed Helledahl.

The captain floated in the air, a ludicrous parody of officerlike erectness. But there was an odd dignity to him all the same.

"I'm sorry," he repeated. "I have a family too, you know. I would turn about if it could be done with reasonable safety. But Professor Winge has shown that that is impossible. We would die anyhow—and our ship would be a ruin, a few bits of worn and crumpled metal, all our results gone. If we proceed, we can prepare specimens and keep records which will be of use to our successors. Us they will find, for we can improvise a conspicuous feature on the hull that the barnacles won't obliterate."

He looked from one to another.

"Shall we do less for our country's honor than the Chinese did for theirs?" he finished.

Well, if you put it that way, thought Bull, yes.

But he couldn't bring himself to say it aloud. Maybe they all thought the same, including Langnes himself, but none was brave enough to admit it. The trouble with us moral cowards, thought Bull, is that we make heroes of ourselves.

I suppose Marta will shed some pretty, nostalgic tears when she gets the news. Ech! It's bad enough to croak out here; but if that bluestocking memorializes me with a newspaper poem about my Viking spirit—

Maybe that's what we should rig up on the hull, so they won't ignore this poor barnacled derelict as just another flying boulder. Make the Holy Ole into a real, old-fashioned, Gokstad type ship. Dragon figurehead, oars, sail . . . shields hung along the side . . . hey, yes! Imagine some smug Russian on an Earth satellite, bragging about how his people were the first into space—and then along comes this Viking ship—

I think I'll even paint the shields. A face on each one, with its tongue out and a thumb to its nose—

Holy hopping Ole!

"Shields!" roared Bull.

"What?" said Langnes through the echoes.

"We're shielded! We can turn back! Right now!"

When the hubbub had died down and a few slide rule calculations had been made, Bull addressed the others.

"It's really quite simple," he said. "All the elements of the answer were there all the time. I'm only surprised that the Chinese never realized it; but then, I imagine they used all their spare moments for socialist self-criticism.

"Anyhow, we know our ship is a space barnacle's paradise. Even our barnacles have barnacles. Why? Because it picks up so much sand and gravel. Now what worried us about heading straight home was not an occasional meteorite big enough to punch clear through the skin of the ship—we've patching to take care of that—no, we were afraid of a sandblast wearing the entire hull paper thin. But we're protected against precisely that danger! The more such little particles that hit us, the more barnacles we'll have. They can't be eroded away, because they're alive. They renew themselves from the very stuff that strikes them. Like a stone in a river, worn away by the current, while the soft moss is always there.

"We'll get back out of the Belt before the radiation level builds up to anything serious. Then, if we want to, we can chisel off the encrustation. But why bother, really? We'll soon be home."

"No argument there," smiled Langnes.

"I'll go check the engines prior to starting up," said Bull. "Will you and Torvald compute us an Earthward course?"

He started for the doorway, paused, and added slowly: "Uh, I kind of hate to say this, but those barnacles are what will really make the Asteroid Belt available to men."

"What?" said Helledahl.

"Sure," said Bull. "Simple. Naturally, we'll have to devise protection for the radio, and redesign the radiation screen apparatus, as the skipper remarked. But under proper control, the barnacles make a self-repairing shield against sandblast. It shouldn't be necessary to go through the Belt on these tedious elliptical orbits. The space miners can take hyperbolic paths, as fast as they choose, in any direction they please.

"I," he finished with emphasis, "will not be among them."

"Where will you be?" asked Winge.

But Erik Bull was already headed aft to his work. A snatch of song, bawled from powerful lungs, came back to the others. They all knew English, but it took them a moment to get the drift.

> "'. . . Who's that knocking at my door?'
> Said the fair young maiden.
> 'Oh, it's only me, from over the sea,'
> Said Barnacle Bill the sailor.
> 'I've sailed the seas from shore to shore,
> I'll never sail the seas no more.
> Now open up this blank-blank door!'
> Said Barnacle Bill the sailor."

JOIN OUR GANG?

By Sterling E. Lanier

Commander William Powers, subleader of Survey Group Sirian Combine—1027798 and hence first officer of its ship, the *Benefactor,* stared coldly out of his cabin port. The *Benefactor* was resting on the bedrock of Island Twenty-seven of the world called Mureess by its natives. Like all the other such names, it meant "the world," just as the natives' name for themselves, Falsethsa, meant "the people," or "us," or "the only race." To Commander Powers, fifty years old, with eleven of them in Survey work, the world was Planet Two of a star called something unpronounceable in the nebula of something else equally pointless. He had not bothered to learn the native name of Island Twenty-seven, because his ship had mapped one thousand three hundred and eighty-six islands, all small, and either rocky or swampy or both. Island Twenty-seven, to him, had only one importance, and that was its being the site of the largest city on the planet.

Around the island's seven square miles, a maze of docks, buildings, sheds, breakwaters, and artificial inlets made a maze stretching a mile out to sea in every direction. The gray sea, now covered with fog patches, rolled on the horizon under low-lying cloud. Numerous craft, some small, some large, moved busily about on the water, which in its com-

ponents was identical with that of Terra, far distant in the
Sirius Sector. Crude but workable atomic motors powered
most of them, and there was a high proportion of submarines. Powers thought of Earth's oceans for a moment,
but then dismissed the thought. Biological technical data
were no specialty he needed. Terra might be suitable for the
action formulating in his mind, but a thousand suns of
Sirian Combine might prove more useful. The biologists of
Grand Base would determine, assisted by data his ship provided, in their monster computers, what was called for.
Powers had been trained for different purposes.

He was, as every survey commander was, a battle-
hardened warrior. He had fought in two major fleet actions
in his day, and had once, as a very junior ensign of the
Sirian Grand Fleet, participated in the ultimate horror, the
destruction by obliteration of an inhabited planet. For
planetary destruction a unanimous vote of the Sirian
Grand Council, representing over four thousand worlds, was
necessary. It had been given only four times in the long
history of the Confederacy. Every intelligent being in the
great Union shuddered at the thought of its ever becoming
necessary again. Powers stared moodily over the rocky
ground toward a group of figures in the distance which were
moving in his direction. The final delegation of the Mureess
government, a world government, was coming for its last
meeting before the *Benefactor* departed into the far reaches
of space.

Powers braced himself mentally for a grand effort. He
held equivalent rank to that of a Galactic admiral, and it
was held for one reason only, because of his real work and
its importance. He was a super-psychologist, a trend-ana-
lyzer, a salesman, a promoter, a viewer, an expert on alien

symbology and the spearhead of the most ruthless intelligence service in the known universe. Long ago, he had transferred from the battle fleet to the inner school at Sirius Prime for the most intensive training ever devised. Now it would be put to the ultimate test.

He heard the air lock open and turned away from the window. He had a long way to walk to the neutral council chamber, for the *Benefactor* was a big ship, despite the fact that only twenty beings comprised the total complement. Down the echoing corridors he paced, brow furrowed in thought. Mazechazz would have his own ideas, he knew, but if they made no impression, he would have to put his oar in. Each being on board, whether he breathed halogen or oxygen, ate uranium or protein, had to be independent in thought and action under certain circumstances. The circumstances were here, here and now in his judgment.

He arrived at the door of the Council chamber, and entered, an impressive sight in flaming orange and blue uniform.

Four members of the Supreme Council of Mureess rose solemnly and inclined their heads in his direction. They were tall bipeds of vaguely reptilian ancestry, most of their height being body. They stood on short powerful legs, terminating in flippered feet, and their long arms were flanged to the second elbow with a rubbery fin. Only four opposed fingers flexed the hands, but the dome-shaped heads and golden eyes screamed intelligence as loudly as the bodies shouted adaption to an aquatic environment. Around the brown torsos, light but efficient harness supported a variety of instruments in noncorrosive metal sheaths. All of the instruments had been discreetly examined by scanning beams and pronounced harmless before any contact had been allowed.

Across the central table, Sakh Mazechazz, of Lyra 8, leader and captain of the Survey stared red-eyed at his executive officer. Mazechazz resembled the delegation far more than he did his own officer, for he, too, had remotely reptilian forbears. Indeed he still sported a flexible tail and, save for his own orange and blue uniform, ablaze with precious stones, resembled nothing so much as a giant Terrestrial chameleon. The uniforms were no accident. Surveymen wore anything or nothing as the case called for it, and the Falsethsa admired bright colors, having few of their own and a good color sense. The gleaming jewels on Mazechazz's uniform stressed his superiority in rank to Powers, as they were meant to.

Of the twenty Surveymen on board the *Benefactor*, Mazechazz and Powers were the only two who most resembled, in that order, the oxygen-breathing natives of Mureess. That automatically made them captain and executive officer of the *Benefactor*. The native population saw only the captain and executive officer of the ship, and only the council chamber. On a world of ammonia breathers, Mazechazz and Powers would have been invisible in their own part of the ship providing advice only to the Skorak of Marga 10, Lambdem, and perhaps Nyur of Antares-bi-12. If a suspicious native saw an entity with whom he could feel a remote relationship giving orders to a weird-looking, far more, alien creature, a feeling of confidence might appear.

Since Mazechazz came from a planet of super-heated desert and scrub resembling the Karoo of South Africa, the resemblance could have been bettered, but it was well within the allowable limits set forth in the Inner Mandate. And in Galactic Psychology, every trick counted. For persuasion was the chief weapon of the Sirian Combine. Outright force was absolutely forbidden, save by the aforesaid vote of the council. Every weapon in the book of persuasion was used to bring intelligent races into the Combine, and persuasion is a thing of infinite variety.

As these thoughts flashed through Powers' mind, he seated himself in a plain chair and adjusted the Universal Speaker to his mouth. Beside him, on a more elaborate chair, tailored to fit his tail, Mazechazz did the same, while the four Falsethsa seated themselves on low stools and took similar instruments from the oblong table which separated them from the two Surveymen. Deep in the bowels of the ship, a giant translator switched on, to simultaneously translate and record the mutually alien tongues as they were spoken. Adjustable extensions on the speakers brought the sound to the bone of the skull. For different life forms, different instruments would have been necessary and were provided for.

Mazechazz, as "captain," opened the proceedings.

"Since this is our last session with you, we hope some fresh proposals have occurred to your honorable council during your absence," hummed the speaker through Powers' skull.

He who was designated First among the council of Mureess answered.

"We have no new proposals, nor indeed had we ever any. Trade would be welcome, but we vitally need nothing you or your Combine have described, captain. We have all the minerals we need and the Great Mother—he meant the sea

—provides food. We will soon go into space ourselves and meet as equals with you. We cannot tolerate what you call an 'observer,' who seems to us a spy, and not subject to our laws by your own definition. That is all we have to say."

That does it, thought Powers glumly. The cold—and entirely accurate—description of a Planetary representative of the Sirian Combine was the final clincher. The intensely proud and chauvinistic Falsethsa would tolerate no interference.

Mazechazz gave no indication that he had heard. He tried again.

"In addition to trade and education, general advancement of the populace," murmured the mike, "have you considered defense?" He paused. "Not all races who travel in space are friendly. A few are starkly inimical, hating all other forms of life. Could you defend yourselves, Honorable Sirs, against such?"

It was obvious from the speed of the answer that the Council of Mureess had considered, if not anticipated this question. The second member spoke, an obvious pre-assignment.

"In all our long history, you are our first contact with star travelers. Yet we are not defenseless. The Great Mother contains not only food, fish and plants which we harvest, but many strong and terrible beasts. Very few are left to disturb us. In addition, the implications of your ship have not escaped us, and our scientists are even now adapting some of our atomic devices used in mining to other ends." The voice contained a faint hint of pride as it ended. We got guns, too, buddy, it said, and we ain't pushovers.

The First of the Council spoke again. "Let me be plain, Respected Star-farers. It seems obvious to us that you have learned most of what we represent as a council, if not all. We are the heads of the Great Clans and we will not change. It hardly seems likely that you represent a society based on heredity if you include the diverse and nameless breeds of creature you have shown us on your screens. We do not want such an amalgam on our world causing unrest and disturbances of public order. Still less do we desire authoritarian interference with the ordered life we have developed. Your requests are one and severally refused. There will be no 'observer.' Trade, regulated by us, will be welcome. Otherwise, should you choose not to be bound by our laws, we must respectfully and finally bid you farewell. When at some future date, we develop ships such as yours, we may reconsider." The speaker paused, looked at his three confreres, who nodded silently. The First stared arrogantly at Mazechazz, and continued.

"Finally, we have decided to place a ban on further landings by aliens unless you are now prepared to negotiate a trade agreement on our terms!"

Powers thought frantically, his face motionless. This was defeat, stark and unequivocal. The parable he had in mind seemed indicated now or never. He turned to Sakh Mazechazz, and spoke.

"May I have your permission to address the Honored Council, Noble Captain?" he asked.

"Speak, First Officer," said the Lyran, his gular pouches throbbing. His ruby eyes, to his associate, looked pained, as well they might.

"Let me pose a question, Honored Sirs," said Powers. "Suppose that in your early history of creating your orderly realm you had discovered on one of your islands a race of

Falsethsa as advanced and regulated as yourselves who wished nothing to do with you?" He could feel the alerted tension of the four as the golden eyes glowed at him.

"The implications of your question are obvious," the First of the Council spoke, as coldly as ever. "Do you threaten us with force from your Combine devoted to peace?" The flat voice of the translator hummed with acquired and impossible violence which Powers knew to be subjective.

The First continued. "We would resist to the ultimate, down to the least of our young and the most helpless female weed cultivator! Do your worst!"

Powers sat back. He had done his best. The hereditary dictatorship of a united world had spoken. No democratic minority had ever raised its head here. The society of Mureess was stratified in a way ancient India never thought of being, down to refuse collectors of a thousand generations of dishonorable standing. Ancient Japan had been as rigidly exclusionist but there *had* been a progressive element there. Here there was nothing. Nothing that is, except a united world of coldly calculating and very advanced entities about to erupt into space with Heaven knew what weapons and a murderous arrogance and race pride to bolster them.

He thought of the dead orb called Sebelia, rolling around its worthless sun, an object of nausea to all life. And he had helped. Well, the boys in Biology had the ball now. He forced himself to listen to the First of Council as he bade Mazechazz a courteous farewell.

"Depart in harmony and peace, Honorable Star-farers. May your Great Mother be benign, when you return to give your high council our message on the far-distant worlds you have shown us in the sky."

The Council departed, leaving Powers and Mazechazz

staring at each other in the council chamber, their gaudy uniforms looking a little dull and drab.

"Well, Sakh," said Powers, his ruddy face a little flushed, "we can't be perfect. They don't know about spacewarps and instantaneous communicators. Plan II has nothing to do with us."

"Beyond our recommendation, you mean," said the Lyran flatly. "We have failed, William. This means death for thousands of innocent beings, perhaps more. Their world population is about eighty million, you know."

There was silence in the room until Powers broke it again.

"Would you have Sebelia, Sakh," he asked gently, "or Ruller I, Bellevan's world, or Labath?" There was no answer to this and he knew it. There was only one alternative to a dead, burned-out, empty planet. Mureess was in the wrong stage of development, and it would have to be brought in line. The Sirian Combine had to, and would remove any intelligent unknown menace from a position from which it could threaten its Master plan of integrated peace. As they left the chamber, Powers said a silent prayer and touched the tiny Crescent and Star embroidered on his shirt pocket. At least, he thought, the planted ultra-wave communicators would be there when the Falsethsa needed them. He looked out of a corridor port at the gray and rolling sea. The Great Mother, he thought bitterly, benevolent and overflowing!

Traleres-124, female gardener, aged thirty-two cycles, hummed in a minor key as she harvested weed of the solstice crop, twelve miles off the northern islands. A rest period was due in the next cycle day, and she and her mate were ahead of quota which should make the supervisor give them a good holiday.

The tall weed swayed gently against her and several small fish darted past in fright. As the first heavy beat of the water struck against her slim body, she looked up. Frozen with horror, she released her container, but in forty feet of water, the monster caught her before she had moved a hundred yards.

As it fed, horribly, other grim shapes, attracted by the blood moved in from the distant murk of deeper water.

Savathake-er rode his one-man torpedo alertly as he probed the southern bay of Ramasarett. He was a scientist-12 and also a hereditary hunter. If the giant fish, long since eliminated from the rest of the seas, were breeding in some secret area of the far and desolate southern rocks, it was his business to know it. No fish could catch his high-powered torpedo, while his electric spears packed a lethal jolt. Probably, he thought, a rumor of the poor fisher folk who worked the southern fringe areas. What else could you expect from such types, who had never even learned to read in a thousand cycles. Nevertheless, as he patrolled the sunken rocks, he was alert, scanning the water on all sides constantly for the great shape he sought, his skin alert for the first strange vibration. By neglecting the broken bottom, brown with laminaria and kelp, he missed the great, mottled tentacle which plucked him off his torpedo in a flash of movement, leaving the riderless craft to cruise aimlessly away into the distance.

"Your highness," said the Supervisor Supreme, "we are helpless. We have never used metal nets, because we have never had to. Our fiber nets they slash to ribbons. They attack every species of food-fish from the Ursaa to the Krad. The breeding rate is fantastic, and now my equal who controls the mines says they are attacking the miners despite all the protection he can give them. They are not large, but in millions—"

"Cease your outcries," said the First in Council, wearily, "and remove that animal from my writing desk. I have seen many pictures of it since they first appeared five cycles ago. It still looks alien and repulsive."

They stared in silence at the shape that any high-school biology student of distant Terra could have identified in his sleep.

At length, the First in Council dismissed the Supervisor of Fisheries and headed thoughtfully for an inner room of his palace. He knew at last the meaning of the strange metal communicating devices, discovered and confiscated after the star ship had departed, six cycles before. It was a simple machine to operate, and he guessed food could be sent incredibly quickly to his starving planet. Just as quickly as other things, he thought grimly. And we have to beg. Hah. Admission to the great peace-loving Combine, may the crabs devour them.

But he knew that he would send and that they would come.

"I was comparing the two reports, my friend," said Mazechazz, "but I am not so familiar with your planetary ecology as I should be. When Mureess applied for admission to the Combine, I requested a copy of their secret directive from Biology, but I had never seen the older report until you gave it to me just now. Can you explain the names to me, if I read them off?"

"Go ahead," said Powers, sipping his sherbet noisily. He seldom wondered what alcohol would feel like any longer. Most Old Believers had tried it when young and disliked it.

"I've already looked up the names I didn't know," he said, "so start the Mureessan list first."

"Great White Shark, or Maneater," read Mazechazz. "He sounds obvious and nasty."

"He is," said Powers. He put down his glass. "Remember, as usual, the birth rate has been at least tripled. An increased metabolism means increased food consumption, and no shark on Terra was ever full. This brute runs forty feet when allowed, in size, that is. A giant carnivorous fish, very tough."

"Number two is Architeuthis, or Giant Squid," continued the Lyran. "Is that a fish? Sorry, but on my world, well, fish are curiosities."

"It's an eyed, carnivorous mollusk with enormous arms, ten of them and it reaches eighty feet long at least. Swims well, too."

There was a moment of silence, then Mazechazz continued. "Smooth dogfish."

"A tiny shark," said Powers, "about three and a half feet in size. They school in thousands on Terra and eat anything that swims. Just a blind agile appetite. They have a high *normal* breeding rate."

"Finally we have a Baleran Salamander, so you're free of one curse, anyway. Balera, I believe, is hellishly wet, although I don't know much about it."

Powers rose and stretched. "He's a little fellow with six legs and a leathery hide. A nuisance on Balera, which is the equivalent of a Terran swamp. He eats every vegetable known, dry or fresh, and, being only two inches long is hard to see. He doesn't bite, just eats things and breeds. There must be millions by now, on each island of Mureess. Then the eggs get carried about. They're tough and adhesive. You can guess what their warehouses looked like."

"At least two million starved before the Council gave in," resumed the Lyran sadly. "But they gave in all the way and abolished caste privilege before the first relief ship even arrived. They'll be full members shortly. And this older report?"

"Read the names," said Powers. He was staring out of the Club window at the stars. "They fed us our own dirt, because we hadn't eliminated all our competitors. Disease means microorganisms, so you choose the largest animal possible with efficiency, that is. Just read the list. My grandparents died, you know, but it had to be done, or we'd have destroyed ourselves. The Combine was a far greater blessing to us than it ever was to Mureess, I can assure you of that!"

He listened in silence as the Lyran read.

"Desmodus, the vampire bat,
Rattus Norvegicus, the common rat,
Mus Domesticus, the common mouse,
The Common Locust,
Sylvilagus, the Cottontail Rabbit,
Passer Domesticus, the House Sparrow,
Sturnus Vulgarus, the European Starling."

Powers sat down and stared at his friend. "Terran life by comparison with many other worlds is terribly tough because we have so many different environments, I suppose. Hence its use on Mureess. Of course, the Combine increased breeding rates again, but adapting that bat to stand cold was the last straw," he said. "The rest of them were all ready and waiting, but the bat was tropical. We'll start with him. Desmodus is a small flying mammal about . . ."

SLEIGHT OF WIT

By Gordon R. Dickson

It was a good world. It was a very good world—well worth a
Class A bonus. Hank Shallo wiped his lips with the back
of one square, hairy, big-knuckled hand, put his coffee cup
down; and threw his ship into orbit around the place. The
orbit had a slight drift to it because the gyros needed over-
hauling; but Hank was used to their anomalies, as he was
to the fact that the coffee maker had to be set lower on the
thermostat than its direction called for. He made automatic course corrections while he looked the planet over
for a place to sit down.

Hank was a world-scout—an interstellar pioneer far-
flung in his fleet one-man spacecraft in search of new homes
for humanity. He had been picked to model as such for a
government publicity release the last time he had been
back to Earth. The picture that resulted, in three-dimensional full-color, showed Hank barrel-chested in a fitted
blue uniform, carelessly open at the throat, seated at the
gleaming controls of a scout cabin mock-up. Utilitarianly
tidy, the little cabin surrounded him, from the folded up
Pullman-type bunk to the arms rack with well-oiled weapons
gleaming on their hooks. A battered guitar leaned in one
corner.

True life showed differences—Hank, barrel-chested in a

pair of khaki shorts, seated at the somewhat rubbed-down controls of the *Andnowyoudont*. Utilitarianly untidy, the little cabin surrounded him, from the anchored down and unmade bunk to the former arms rack, with well-oiled spade, ax, post-hole digger, wire-clippers, et cetera, hanging from the hooks. (In the ammunition locker were five sticks of non-issue dynamite. Hank, when talking shop on his infrequent trips back home, was capable of waxing lyrical over dynamite. "A tool," he would call it, "—a weapon. It'll dig for you, fight for you, run a bluff for you. The only thing it won't do for you is cook the meals and make the bunk.")

A battered guitar leaned in one corner.

On the ninth time around, Hank had complete surface maps of the world below. He ran them back through the ship's Library and punched for that spot on one of the world's three continents where landing conditions were optimum. Then he turned everything over to the automatic pilot and took a little nap.

When instinct woke him up, *Andnowyoudont* was just balancing herself in for a landing in a little meadow surrounded by trees and pleasant-looking enough to be park-like. What hint of warning it was that reached him in the midst of his slumber he was never to know; but one moment he was asleep—and the next he was halfway to the control panel.

Then concussion slammed the ship like a giant's hand. He tripped, caught one glimpse of the near wall of the cabin tilting at him, and consciousness dissolved in one of the prettiest displays of shooting stars he had seen in some time.

He woke again—this time to a throbbing headache and a

lump on his forehead. He sat up groggily, hoisted himself the rest of the way to his feet and stumped over to the medicine chest, absently noting that the ship was, at least, still upright. The outside screen was on, showing a view of the meadow. Five years before he would have looked out of it immediately. Now he was more interested in aspirin.

When he had the aspirin inside him and had checked to make sure the bump on his head was not bleeding and the guitar had not been damaged he turned at last to the screen, sat down in the pilot chair and swept the outside scanner about the meadow. The meadow turned before him, stopped, and the screen steadied on a tall, gray shape.

At the far end of the meadow was another ship. It was half again as big as the *Andnowyoudont*, it resembled no ship of human manufacture that Hank had ever seen; and it had a sort of metal bubble or turret where its nose should be. From this turret projected a pair of short, blunt wide-mouthed tubes bearing an uncomfortable resemblance to the muzzles of guns. They were pointed directly at the *Andnowyoudont*.

Hank whistled the first three notes of "There'll Be A Hot Time In The Old Town, Tonight"—and broke off rather abruptly. He sat staring out the screen at the alien spaceship.

"Now," he said, after a while to the room around him, "against this—the odds against this happening, both of us here at the same time, in the same place, must be something like ten billion to one."

Which was possibly true. But which also, the saying of it didn't help a bit.

Hank got up rather heavily, went over to the coffee maker, and drew himself a cup of coffee. He sat down in his chair before the controls and examined a bank of tell-tale gauges. Not too much to his surprise, these mechanical watchdogs informed him that the *Andnowyoudont* was being sniffed at by various kinds of radiation. He was careful not to touch anything just yet. The thought of the five sticks of dynamite popped into his head and popped out again. The human race's expansion to the stars had brought them before this into contact with some life forms which might reasonably be called intelligent—but no one before that Hank knew of, in his line of work or out of it, had actually run across what you might call a comparable, *space-going* intelligent race.

"Except now Mrs. Shallo's little boy," said Hank to himself. "Naturally. Of course."

No, it was clearly not a dynamite-solution type problem. The stranger yonder was obviously armed and touchy. The *Andnowyoudont* packed five sticks of dynamite, a lot of useful, peaceful sorts of tools, and Hank. Hank leaned back in his chair, sipped on his coffee and turned the situation over to the one device on the ship that had a tinker's chance of handling it—some fifty ounces of gray matter just abaft his eyebrows and between his ears.

He was working this device rather hard, when the hull of the *Andnowyoudont* began to vibrate at short intervals. The vibration resulted in a series of short hums or buzzes. Hank plugged in to the ship's Library and asked it what it thought of this new development.

"The alien ship appears to be trying to communicate with you," the Library informed him.

"Well, see if you can make any sense out of its code," Hank directed. "But don't answer—not yet, anyway."

He went back to his thinking.

One of the less glamorous aspects of Hank's profession—and one that had been hardly mentioned in the publicity release containing the picture he had modeled for, aforesaid—was a heavy schedule of classes, lectures, and briefing sections he was obligated to attend every time he returned to Headquarters, back on Earth. The purpose of these home chores was to keep him, and others like him, abreast of the latest developments and discoveries that might prove useful to him.

It was unfortunate that this would have meant informing him about practically everything that had happened since his last visit, if the intent had been followed literally. Ideally, a world scout should know everything from aardvark psychology to the Zyrian language. Practically, since such overall coverage was impossible, an effort was made to hit hard only the obviously relevant new information and merely survey other areas of new knowledge.

All new information, of course, was incorporated into the memory crystals of the Library; but the trick from Hank's point of view was to remember what to ask for and how to ask for it. Covered in one of the surveys when he had been back last trip had been a rather controversial theory by somebody or other to the effect that an alien space-going race interested in the same sort of planets as humans were, would not only look a lot like, but act a lot like, humans. Hank closed his eyes.

"Bandits," he recited to himself. "Bayberry, barberry, burberry, buckle—May Sixteenth. Sinuses, shamuses, cyclical, sops—milk-and-bread . . . Library, Walter M. Breadon's 'Speculations on Alien Responses.' "

There was an almost imperceptible delay, and then a screen in front of Hank lit up with a pictured text.

". . . *Let us amuse ourselves now,* (commenced the pictured text) *with a few speculations about the personality and nature of a space-going alien such as one of you might encounter . . .*"

Hank snorted and settled down to read.

Twenty minutes later he had confirmed his remembrance of the fact that Breadon thought that an alien, such as must be in the ship opposite Hank right now, would react necessarily very similarly to a human. Because, Breadon's theory ran, of necessarily parallel environments and past stages of development.

At this moment, the call bell on Hank's deep-space receiver rang loudly.

"What's up?" he asked the Library, keying it in.

"The alien ship has evidently concluded that it can speak to you over normal communication equipment. It is calling the *Andnowyoudont.*"

"Fine," said Hank. "I wonder what the name of Breadon's opposite number is among the aliens."

"I am sorry. I do not have that information."

"Yeah. Well, stand by to translate." Hank keyed in the communicator board. A screen before him lit up with the image of a hairless individual, lacking even eyebrows; with pronounced bony brow ridges, a wide mouth, no chin to speak of, and what appeared to be a turtleneck sweater drawn high on a thick neck.

This individual stared for a long second; and then began to gobble at him. Eventually he ran down and went back to staring again. Hank, his finger still off the send button, turned to the Library.

"What'd he say?"

"I will need more referents. Possibly if you speak now, he will perhaps speak again."

"Not on your life." Hank looked at the alien. The alien looked back. The staring match went on for some time. Abruptly the alien started gobbling again. He gobbled for some time, this time. He also waved a fist in the air. It was a rather slim fist considering the thickness of his neck.

"Well?" demanded Hank of the Library, after the figure in the screen had fallen silent a second time.

"First message: 'You are under arrest.'"

"That's *all* he said?"

"Agglutination appears to be a prime characteristic of his language."

"All right—" growled Hank. "Go on."

"Second message: 'You have offended the responsible authorities and their immediate representative, in the person of I who address you. You are arrested and helpless. Submit therefore immediately or you will be utterly destroyed.'"

Hank thought for a minute.

"Translate," he said to the Library. He pressed the send button. "Tut-tut!" he said to the alien.

"I am unable to translate 'tut-tut,'" said the Library.

"Oh?" Hank grinned. His grin widened. He began to laugh. He laughed louder.

"I am unable to translate laughter," said the Library.

Hank was rolling around in his seat and hiccuping with helpless merriment. He reached out with one hand and slapped the send button to *off*. The screen went dark before him as the still-blankly staring alien faded from view. Whooping, Hank pulled himself to an upright position. Abruptly he stopped.

"What am I doing?" he muttered. "The set's off now." He wiped a damp forehead with the hairy back of one large hand and got up to totter over to one of the food compartments. He opened it and hauled out a large brown bottle.

Liquor was not a normal part of the supply list on scout ships—for reasons of space, rather than those of sobriety, a drinking world scout being a sort of self-canceling problem. On the other hand, a closed cycle that reprocessed waste matter of an organic nature and started it around again to become food required efficient little manufactories that were quite as capable of turning out ersatz beer as ersatz steak. The result was that world scouts were beer drinkers if they were any sort of drinkers at all.

They were also the despair of waiters, waitresses, and bartenders. A group of world scouts spending a social moment together would order a bottle apiece of cold beer; drain their bottles, when they came, in a couple of seconds; and then sit with the empty bottles before them, refusing to reorder until about forty-five minutes had passed. Then the whole process would be repeated.

A world scout determined to get drunk merely shortened the interval between bottles. One determined to stay cold sober, while appearing to drink, lengthened it. A member of the laity, sitting in with them on these sessions, was normally destroyed—either by drink or frustration.

In this particular case Hank flipped the seal off the top of the bottle in his hand, poured half a liter of beer down his throat, carefully resealed the bottle and put it back in its refrigerator compartment. He then carefully counted the remaining full containers of beer in the compartment and set the beer-producing controls on high.

After this he was almost attacked by another spasm of laughter, but he fought it down. He went over to the desk of controls and flicked on an outside screen. It lit up with a view of the meadow with the afternoon sun beaming down on the soft grass and the tall gunmetal-colored shape of the alien ship.

"A beautiful day," said Hank aloud, "for a picnic."

"Do you wish me to make a note of that fact?" inquired the Library, which had been left on.

"Why not?" said Hank. He went cheerfully about the room, opening lockers and taking things out. A sudden thought occurred to him. He went across to the desk controls to check the readings on certain instruments concerned with the physical environment of the world outside—but these gave the meadow a clean bill of health. He added the full bottles of beer to his pile, enclosing them in a temperature bag, and headed out the air lock of his ship.

Reaching the ground outside, he proceeded to a comfortable spot on the grass and about midway between his ship and that of the alien.

Half an hour later, he had a cheerful small fire going in the center of a small circle of stones, a hammock hung on wooden posts, and small conveniences such as a beer-cooler and an insulated box of assorted snacks within easy reach. He lay in the hammock and strummed his guitar and sang. He also swallowed a half liter of beer approximately every thirty-five minutes.

The beer did nothing to improve his voice. There was a

reason Hank Shallo sang while off on his lonely trips of exploration—no civilized community could endure the horrendousness of his vocal cords when these vibrated in song. By a combination of bribery and intimidation he had forced an indigent music instructor once to teach him how to stay in key. So, stay in key he did; but the result was still a sort of bass bray capable of penetrating six-inch walls and rattling windows.

The alien ship showed no sign of life.

As the sun began slowly to drown itself in twilight, however, Hank became aware to his pleasant surprise that the local inhabitants of this world did not seem to join most of the rest of the galaxy in its disdain for his singing. An assortment of small animals of various shapes and sizes had gathered around his camping spot and sat in a circle. He was not unduly surprised, what with the beer he had drunk and all, when after a little while one of the larger creatures—a sort of rabbit-shaped beast sitting up on its hind legs—began to harmonize with him.

If Hank's voice had somewhat the sonority of a cross-cut saw, the beast's had the pure liquidity of an angel's. They were rendering a remarkable performance, albeit four octaves apart—and it had grown rather dark—when a blinding light burst suddenly into being from the top of the alien ship. It washed the meadow in a brilliance like that of an atomic flare; and the native animals took to their heels. Sitting up in the hammock and blinking, Hank saw the alien approaching him on foot. The alien was pushing a black box the size of a suitcase on two wheels. He trundled it up to the campfire, hitched up the floppy, black, bell-bottomed trousers which supplemented the turtle-necked upper garment Hank had remarked on the screen earlier, and gobbled at Hank.

"Sorry, buddy," said Hank. "I haven't got my translator with me."

The alien gobbled some more. Hank idly strummed a few stray chords and regretted the fact that he hadn't gotten the native animal to harmonizing with him on "Love's Old Sweet Song," which would have been ideally suited to their two voices together.

The alien stopped gobbling and jabbed one finger—somewhat angrily, it seemed to Hank, down on a button on top of the black box. There was a moment's hesitation; then he gobbled again and a curiously flat and unaccented English came out of the box.

"You are under arrest," it said.

"Think again," said Hank.

"What do you mean?"

"I mean I refuse to be arrested. Have a drink?"

"If you resist arrest, I will destroy you."

"No, you won't."

"I assure you I will."

"You can't," said Hank.

The alien looked at him with an expression that Hank took to be one of suspicion.

"My ship," said the alien, "is armed and yours is not."

"Oh, you mean those silly little weapons in your ship's nose?" Hank said. "They're no good against me."

"No good?"

"That's right, brother."

"We are not even of the same species. Do not allow your ignorance to lead you into the error of insulting me. To amuse myself, I will ask you why you are under the illusion that the most powerful scientific weapons known have no power against you?"

"I have," said Hank, "a greater weapon."

The alien looked at him suspiciously a second time.

"You are a liar," the box said, after a moment.

"Tut-tut," said Hank.

"What was that last noise you made? My translator does not yet recognize it."

"And it never will."

"This translator will sooner or later recognize every word in your language."

"Not a geepfleish word like *tut-tut*."

"What kind of a word?" It might, thought Hank, be merely false optimism on his part; but he thought the alien was beginning to look a little uncertain.

"Geepfleish—words dealing with the Ultimate Art-Science."

The alien hesitated for a third time.

"To get back to this fantastic claim of yours to having a weapon—what kind of weapon could be greater than a nuclear cannon capable of destroying a mountain?"

"Obviously," said Hank. "The Ultimate Weapon."

"The . . . Ultimate Weapon?"

"Certainly. The weapon evolved on Ultimate Art-Science principles."

"What kind of a weapon," said the alien, "is that?"

"It's quite impossible to explain," said Hank, airily, "to someone having no understanding of the Ultimate Art-Science."

"May I see this weapon?"

"You ain't capable of seeing it, kid," said Hank.

"If you will demonstrate its power to me," said the alien, after a pause, "I will believe your claim."

"The only way to demonstrate it would be to use it on you," said Hank. "It only works on intelligent life forms."

He reached over the edge of his hammock and opened another beer. When he set the half-empty bottle down again the alien was still standing there.

"You are a liar," the alien said.

"A crude individual like you," said Hank, delicately wiping a fleck of foam from his upper lip with the back of one hairy hand, "would naturally think so."

The alien turned abruptly and trundled his translator back toward his ship. A few moments later, the overhead light went out and the meadow was swallowed up in darkness except for the feeble light of the fire.

"Well," said Hank, getting up out of the hammock and yawning, "I guess that's that for today."

He took the guitar and went back to his ship. As he was going back in through the air lock, he thought he felt something about the size of a mouse scurry over his foot; and he caught a glimpse of something small, black and metallic that slipped out of sight under the control desk as he looked at it.

Hank grinned rather foolishly at the room about him and went to bed.

He woke once during the night; and lay there listening. By straining his ears, he could just occasionally make out a faint noise of movements. Satisfied, he went back to sleep again.

Early morning found him out of bed and humming to himself. He flipped the thermostat on the coffee maker up for a quick cup, set up the cabin thermostat and opened both doors of the air lock to let in the fresh morning air. Then he drew his cup of coffee, lowered the thermostat on the coffee maker again and keyed in the automatic broom. The broom scurried about, accumulating a small heap of dust and minor rubble, which it dumped outside the air lock. In the heap, Hank had time to notice, were a number of tiny mobile mechanical devices—like robot ants. Still drinking his coffee, he went over to the drawer that held the operating manual for ships of the class of *Andnowyoudont.* Holding it up by the binding; he shook it. A couple more of the tiny devices fell out; and the automatic broom, buzzing —it seemed to Hank—reproachfully, scurried over to collect them.

Hank was fixing himself breakfast, when the screen announced he was being called from the other ship. He stepped over and answered. The image of the alien lit up on the screen.

"You have had the night to think things over," said the flat voice of the alien's translator. "I will give you twelve point three seven five nine of your minutes more in which to surrender you and your ship to me. If you have not surrendered by the end of that time, I will destroy you."

"You could at least wait until I've had breakfast," said Hank. He yawned, and shut off the set.

He went back to fixing his breakfast, whistling as he did so. But the whistle ran a little flat; and he found he was keeping one eye on the clock. He decided he wasn't hungry after all, and sat down to watch the clock in the control desk as its hands marked off the seconds toward the deadline.

Nothing happened, however. When the deadline was a good several minutes past, he let out a relieved sigh and unclenched his hands, which he found had been maintaining quite a grip on the arms of his chair. He went back and had breakfast after all.

Then he set the coffee maker to turn itself on as soon as he came in, got down some fresh reading material from the top shelf of his bookcase—giving his head a rather painful bang on the fire-control sprinkler overhead, in the process— and stopped to rub his head and swear at the sprinkler. He then comforted himself with the last cup of coffee that was still in the coffee maker, unplugged the emergency automatic controls so that the air-lock doors would stay open while he was out, loaded himself up with beer—but left the reading material roosting on top of the coffee maker—and went out to his hammock.

Forty minutes and a liter and a half of beer later, he was again in a good mood. He took an ax into the nearby woods and began chopping poles for a lean-to. By lunch-time his hammock was swinging comfortably in the shade of the lean-to, his guitar was in tune, and his native audience was gathering again. He sang for about an hour, the small, rabbitlike creature harmonizing with parrotlike faithfulness to the tune, and had lunch. He was just about to take a small nap in the hammock when he saw the alien once more trundling his translator in the direction of the camp.

He reached the fireplace and stopped. Hank sat up with his legs over the edge of the hammock.

"Let us talk," said the alien.

"Fine," said Hank.

"I will be frank."

"Fine."

"And I will expect you to be frank."

"Why not?"

"We are both," said the alien, "intelligent beings of a high level of scientific culture. In spite of the apparent differences between us, we actually have a great deal in common. We must consider first the amazing coincidence that caused us both to land on the same world at the same spot at the same time—"

"Not so much of a coincidence," said Hank.

"What do you mean?" The alien all but glowered at him.

"It stands to reason," Hank leaned back comfortably in the hammock and caught hold of his knee with both hands to balance himself. "Your people and mine have probably been pretty close to bumping into each other all along. They've probably been close to each other a ·number of times before. But space is pretty big. Your ship and mine could easily zip right by each other a thousand times and never be noticed by one another. The most logical place to bump into each other *is* on a planet we both want. As for coming down in the same place—I set my equipment to pick out the most likely landing spot. I suppose you did the same?"

"It is not my function," said the alien, "to give you information."

"It isn't necessary for you to, either," grunted Hank. "It's pretty obvious your native star and mine aren't too far apart as galactic distances go—and our exploratory ships have been getting closer to the opposing home worlds all the time. Instead of it being such a coincidence, you might say our meeting was close to inevitable." He cocked an eye at the alien. "And I'm sure you've already figured that out for yourself as well as I did."

The alien hesitated for a moment.

"I see," he said at last, "there is no point in my trying to deceive you."

"Oh you can *try* if you like," said Hank, generously.

"No, I will be absolutely frank."

"Suit yourself."

"You obviously have assessed the situation here as fully and correctly as I have myself. Here we stand, facing each other in an armed truce. There can be no question of either of us allowing the other to carry word of the other's civilization back to his own people. We cannot take the chance that the other's people are not inimical and highly dangerous. It becomes, therefore, the duty of each of us to capture the other." He cocked an eye at Hank. "Am I correct?"

"You're doing the talking," said Hank.

"At the present moment, we find ourselves at an impasse. My ship is possessed of a weapon which, by all the laws of science, should be able to destroy your ship utterly. Logically, you are at my mercy. However, illogically, you deny this."

"Yep," said Hank.

"You lay claim to an invisible weapon which you claim is greater than my own, and puts me at your mercy. For my own part I believe you are lying. But for the sake of my people I cannot put the matter to a test as things now stand. If I should do so and it should turn out I was wrong, I would be responsible for calamity."

"Yes, indeed," said Hank.

"However, an area of doubt remains in my mind. If you are so sure of the relative superiority of your weapon, why have you hesitated to make me prisoner in your turn?"

"Why bother?" Hank let go of his knee and leaned forward confidentially with both feet on the ground. "To be frank right back at you—you're harmless. Besides, I'm going to settle down here."

"Settle down? You mean you are going to set up residence here?"

"Certainly. It's my world."

"Your world?"

"Among my people," said Hank, loftily, "when you find a world you like that no one else of our own kind has already staked out, you get to keep it."

The pause the alien made this time was a very long one indeed.

"Now I know you are a liar," he said.

"Well, suit yourself," said Hank, mildly.

The alien stood staring at him.

"You leave me no alternative," said the alien at last. "I offer you a proposition. I will give you proof that I have destroyed my cannon, if you will give me proof that you have destroyed your weapon. Then we can settle matters on the even basis that will result."

"Unfortunately," said Hank, "this weapon of mine can't be destroyed."

"Then," the alien backed off a step and started to turn his translator around back toward the ship. "I must take the chance that you are not a liar and do my best to destroy you after all."

"Hey! Hold on a minute!" said Hank. The alien paused and turned back. "Don't rush off like that." Hank stood up and flexed his muscles casually. The two were about the same height but it was obvious Hank carried what would have been an Earthweight advantage of about fifty pounds. "You want to settle this man-to-man, I'm willing. No weapons, no holds barred. There's a sporting proposition for you."

"I am not a savage," retorted the alien. "Or a fool."

"Clubs?" said Hank, hopefully.

"No."

"Knives?"

"Certainly not."

"All right," said Hank, shrugging, "have it your way. Go get yourself destroyed. I did my best to find some way out for you."

The alien stood still as if thinking.

"Let me make you a second proposition," he said at last. "All the alternatives you propose are those which give you the advantage. Let us reverse that. Let me propose that we trade ships, you and I."

"What?" squawked Hank.

"You see? You are not interested in any fair encounter."

"Certainly I am! But trade ships—why don't you just ask me to give up right now?"

"Because you obviously will not do so."

"There's no difference between that and asking me to trade ships!" shouted Hank.

"Who knows?" said the alien. "Possibly you will learn to operate my cannon before I learn to operate your weapon."

"You never could anyway—work mine, that is!" snorted Hank.

"I am willing to take my chances."

"It's ridiculous!"

"Very well." The alien turned away. "I have no alternative but to do my best to destroy you."

"Hold on. Hold on—" said Hank. "Look, all right. I agree.

Just let me go back to my ship for a minute and pick up a few personal—"

"No. Neither one of us can take the chance of the other setting up a trap in his own ship. We trade now—without either of us going back to our ships."

"Well, now look—" Hank took a step toward him.

"Stand back," said the alien. "I am connected with my cannon by remote controls at this moment."

"The air-lock doors to my ship are open. Yours aren't."

The alien reached out and touched the black box. Behind him, the air-lock door of the alien ship swung open, revealing an open inner door and a dark interior.

"I will abandon my translator at the entrance to your ship," said the alien. "Is it settled?"

"Settled!" said Hank. He began walking toward the alien ship, looking back over his shoulder. The alien began trundling his black box toward Hank's ship. As the distance between them widened, they began to put on speed. Halfway to the alien ship, Hank found himself running. He came panting up to the entrance of the alien air lock, and looked back just in time to see the alien dragging his black box in through the air lock of Hank's ship.

"Hey!" yelled Hank, outraged. "You promised—"

The slam of the outer air-lock door, on his own ship, cut him off in mid-protest. He leaned against the open door of the alien ship's air lock, getting his breath back. It occurred to him as a stray thought that he was built for power rather than speed.

"I should have walked," he told the alien ship. "It wouldn't have made any difference." He glanced at his wrist watch. "I'll give him three minutes. He sure didn't lose any time finding those air-lock controls."

He watched the second hand of his watch go around. When it passed the two and a half minute point, he began walking back to his own ship. He reached its closed air-lock door and fumbled with his fingers under the doorframe for the outside lock control button. He found and pressed it.

The door swung open. Smoke spurted out, followed instantly—as the door swung wide—by a flood of water. Washed out on the crest of this escaping flood came a very bedraggled looking alien. He stirred feebly, gargled something at Hank, and collapsed. Inside the spaceship a small torrential shower seemed to be in progress.

Hank hooked one big hand into the alien's turtleneck upper garment and dragged him back into the ship. Groping around in the downpour, he found the controls for the automatic fire sprinkler system and turned them off. The shower ceased. Hank fanned smoke away from in front of his face, stepped across to the coffee maker and turned it off. He punched buttons to start the ventilating system and close the air-lock doors. Then he set about tying the alien to the bunk.

When the alien began to stir, they were already in nullspace, on the first point-to-point jump of the three-day trip that would bring them back to Earth. The alien opened his eyes; and Hank, looking up from his job of repairing the coffee maker, saw the other's stare full upon him.

"Oh!" said Hank. He stopped work, went across the room and brought back the black box on wheels to within reach of the alien's bound hands. The alien reached out and touched it. The box spoke, echoing his gobble.

"What did I do wrong?"

Hank nodded at the coffee maker. He sat down and went

back to work on it. It was in bad shape, having evidently suffered some kind of an explosion.

"I had that set to turn on when I came back in," he said. "Closing the air-lock doors turned it on. Convenient little connection I installed about a year or so back. Only, it just so happened I'd drawn the last cup out of it before I went out. There was just enough moisture in it to cause a steam explosion."

"But the water? The smoke?"

"The automatic sprinkling system," explained Hank. "It reacts to any spot of dangerously high temperature in the room here. When the coffee maker split open, the heating element was exposed. The sprinkling system began flooding the place."

"But the smoke?"

"Some burnable reading material I had on top of the coffee maker. Now that," said Hank, finishing his repairs on the coffee maker, "was something I was absolutely counting on—that the books would fall down onto the burner. And they did." He slapped the coffee maker affectionately and stood up. He looked down at the alien. "Afraid you're going to be somewhat hungry for the next three days or so. But as soon as we get to Earth, you can tell our nutritionists what you eat and they'll synthetize it for you."

He grinned at the other.

"Don't take it so hard," he said. "You'll find we humans aren't all that tough to take when you get to know us."

The alien closed his eyes. Something like a sigh of defeat came from the black box.

"So you had no weapon," it said.

"What do you mean?" said Hank, dropping into the chair

at the control board, indignantly. "Of course I had a weapon."

The eyes of the alien flew wide open.

"Where is it?" he cried. "I sent robots in. They examined this ship of yours right down to the elements that hold it together. They found no weapon. *I* found no weapon."

"You're my prisoner aren't you?" said Hank.

"Of course I am. What of it? What I'm asking is to see your weapon. I could not find it; but you say you still have it. Show it to me. I tell you, I do not see it!"

Hank shook his head sadly; and reached for the controls of the *Andnowyoudont* to set up the next jump.

"Brother," he said. "I don't know. If you don't see it— after all this—then I pity your people when my people really get to know them. That's all I've got to say!"

PROLOGUE TO AN ANALOGUE

By Leigh Richmond

The IWC program was a newscast by Bill Howard, and the news was particularly vicious that night.

Bill, his big homely face leaning across a desk toward the viewer, talked in horrified tones of the "pest-sub" that had reputedly got stuck in the Suez and spread epidemic across Cairo.

It was easy to assume, Bill told his audience, that the nations most interested in creating a crisis in the world right now had put the sub there to make an excuse to accuse us of the terror. It was undoubtedly really there, and was undoubtedly really of American make, and the epidemic was undoubtedly very real indeed, he said. The United Nations investigating team, due to go into the Canal Zone the next day and make their report to the world, would find that the epidemic was caused by laboratory-developed bacteria, carried in by an American-made sub. It would be at least as bad, if not worse, than reported.

The question before the world, Bill said, was not whether bacteriological warfare had started, but who had started it —and the fact that the sub carried United States markings and was of United States make did not at all answer the question.

Bacteriological warfare had broken out and where it would strike next was anybody's guess.

"But let there be no mistake," Bill said. "This is war."

It was on that note that the station break came, and the thirteen witches, trademark of the International Witch Corporation, came on.

Harvey Randolph, manufacturer of the Witch line of products, leaned toward the screen intently. He had just transferred his account to Burton, Dester, Duston & Oswald, and they had dreamed up a new-type commercial for the products.

The thirteen witches were long-legged, slender dancing gals, in tall black witch caps and long black capes, crimson-lined, and very little else. Each had long hair that swirled as she danced.

Randolph chewed his lip, watching them thoughtfully.

They came on with what was almost a valkyrie cry— "Witches of the world, unite—to make it clean, clean, clean, Witch clean—NOW!"

"Hm-m-m," thought Randolph. The cry struck rather sourly at the end of that "this is war" sentence from the newscast, he thought, but then that dramatic newscast-ending was rather unusual.

The witches were singing a jingling chorus as they danced. "No task is too big, no task is too small," they sang. "Which Witch do you need? You should have them all—"

Each witch, of course, displayed her particular product from the Witch line—detergent, soap, shampoo, cleanser, cleaning fluid . . .

"Witch soap or detergent

"Witch cleanser upsurgent . . .

"Which Witch do you need? You should have them all . . ."

This was fairly average as commercials go, thought Randolph. The big BDD&O radical innovation would be next.

It was. On the screen behind the witches appeared a map of the Suez Canal, and then a papier-mâché model of the nose of a sub, and a dockside shanty, a gray pall hanging over them.

As the witches turned and began dancing towards it, the deep voice of the announcer spoke over the muted jingle. "Witches of the world, unite! If Nasser had enough Witches, he could solve the crisis which has us all in stitches . . ."

And the witches, in a united dance-step, approached the sub and shanty singing "Make it clean, clean, clean, Witch clean, NOW!" Each sprayed it with a Witch product, and as they sprayed the pall lifted, the sub and shanty showed shining bright, new-painted.

"Clean, clean, clean," chanted the chorus; "Witch, Witch, Witch, clean, clean, clean. Defy dirt, defy disease.

"Keep Witch clean!"

Well, thought Randolph. And then again, Well.

He wasn't quite sure, he told himself. The commercial came darn near being in poor taste, what with the crisis so near, and yet . . . it wasn't something to make you forget the product. By Geoffery, no! You'd think of Witch products quite a bit, after watching that one.

He reminded himself to check the viewer reaction that would be available fairly early next day, as he switched off the TV.

It was almost noon next day before Randolph reminded

himself of the call he'd planned to make to BDD&O. He got Oswald on the wire almost immediately.

"Randolph, here," he said. "I called you about that new commercial. It seems a little drastic. Are you planning to use it again tonight?"

"Use it? We're taking full credit, in a witchery sort of say!" Oswald laughed. "Never saw anything like your luck, Randolph. I've got the entire staff tied up doing the follow-up for tonight. You needn't worry about libel, either. We've got the whole legal staff turned out, going over every detail."

"It seemed pretty near the line to me," said Randolph, chewing his lip. He found himself a little puzzled over Oswald's tone, but not too much so. Any public relations man was overenthusiastic by nature, in Randolph's estimation. Maybe it took that to make a good p.r. man. "People might resent our making hay out of sickness, even if you are preaching that cleanliness will prevent it."

"Sickness, you might have a point. I admit I'd argue it, but you might. But wellness, now, it's different. I do know that if the United Nations team reports there's no epidemic, and that the pest-sub is one of the cleanest, healthiest-crewed submarines in the business, it's safe for us to assume it's so, and to imply that Witch products are used to keep it clean."

"Mr. Oswald," Randolph's voice took on a note of imperious prissiness. "Would you mind explaining just exactly what you are talking about?"

"Haven't you heard the news? There's no bacteriological war! I admit that puts Bill Howard way out on a limb, but there are a lot of very fine people with him. There's no epidemic in Cairo. There's not even a bad cold that the United

Nations team could find. And they give that so-called pest-sub the most complete bill of health in the business.

"Now, the deal we plan for tonight . . ."

At the same moment, a number of very important people were closeted with the President. Their reactions to the United Nations report were quite otherwise than those Oswald was experiencing.

"It's the exact timing, and the detail of execution that scares me, Mr. President," the Undersecretary of State was saying. The Secretary himself was coming in by jet, and would join them immediately on arrival.

"It implies a technology that we can't touch even in our wildest dreams. I've talked to the CIA chief himself, and the reports from our operatives are beyond question. The epidemic was not only real, it was widespread. The pest-sub was as real as this chair I'm sitting on, and its crew near death to the man, and no question about it.

"If they can fight a bacterial war and produce an overnight cure at the same time . . . we're at their mercy. There is no bomb ever developed—or that can be developed—to touch the power of what they've just demonstrated."

The President ran his fingers through his hair. His face looked more drawn than any man had yet seen it. Yet he smiled.

"We're not suing for peace terms yet," he said, and turned to the nation's foremost biologist, sitting quiet in a nearby chair.

"What's your reaction?" he asked.

"We've always known," the answer came despondently, "that bacteriological warfare is far deadlier than any bomb —if there were any protection from its effects for the victor.

We had a strain of bacteria once, for which we had an immunization course, and we developed it far enough along the line to realize that, even though you immunized every man, woman and child in this country in advance of releasing it in another part of the world, mutant strains would eventually wipe out this nation as well as those we fought."

"How about mutant strains of the Suez bacteria?" the President asked, then answered himself. "No, they've produced an antidote. An antidote, if our reports are correct, that works overnight." He shook his head slowly.

"The ultimatum should come very soon now," the President said.

"It is the timing. I do not understand the timing." The big man in the Kremlin was allowing himself an appearance of indecision that he did not often indulge before underlings.

Of course, there was but the one underling, and any audience that proved to have a later-embarrassing potential could be silenced with ease. Still, it was unusual, and the lieutenant who served as combination secretary and backstop for oratory quaked as he listened.

"The timing is all wrong, but the fact is a fact. It must be a fact, or every operative we have should be Siberianized.

"We must, of course, act. The action must be immediate. We are zeroed in . . ."

"No!" Vlada heard himself speak, and his whole body was outraged at the action. He stood white, trembling. But he had spoken, and try as he would, the word could not be pulled back.

"No? My little dove, and what would you suggest, then, if we are not to defend ourselves from this capitalistic aggression? That we shall sit with our hands folded and allow them to dictate the terms of our surrender? Speak!"

"Send them a pest-sub, and see if they can handle the bacteria we have developed!" Vlada's throat was dry, and his voice was not his own. No power on earth could have made him open his mouth, but he had opened it, and he fully expected the lightning to strike him at that moment.

"Send them . . . ah, of course. They can cure their own, and they have taken a so-dramatic method of saying that they can cure their own. But can they cure the products of our laboratories? Now that, we shall see.

"But we shall be as subtle—more subtle, even, than were our capitalistic friends. We shall not send our sub to them. We shall send it to a small island, and we shall see whether they wish to taste the death, the strangulation and crippling and suffering, the destruction of sanity that shall be the lot of those islanders . . ."

In Peiping the distress was no less acute—but the reaction was somewhat different.

The scientist being grilled had no hope left. He could answer honestly, for there was nothing that could save him from that which was in store.

"The strain was virulent. There is no known antidote— nothing could have saved that port, nor most of Africa and most of India—and there was no way for the world to know from whence came the death-dealing submarine except that it be the mighty America.

"The bombs should have come in retaliation, spreading their death and adding to the impetus of the epidemic, so that enough of the world was wiped out to give the great People of the Dragon room into which to expand. We calculated that a third of our own would be wiped out in the holocaust, which would have relieved us of many problems. The tan peoples of India and the darker peoples of Africa should have sued us to lead them in a unity of the yellow peoples, against the insanities of the pale peoples of the west.

"There is no antidote . . . yet the epidemic is destroyed. I cannot yet believe what is told me. I would go to my ancestors happily if I could go to them with the answer to this riddle."

That night Bill Howard came on the screen his big homely face wreathed in smiles, his tweed suit and shaggy blond hair looking even more informal than usual.

"It's a great day for the people of the world," he said.

"There's undoubtedly tremendous political significance in what happened at Suez, and every statesman and every politician will have statements to make, and conclusions to draw.

"Suez's obvious healthiness has been variously attributed to American technology, garnered from the experts we've sent them over the years; to Russian technology, garnered from their experts loaned to the nation involved; to Mohammed and to the God of the Christians.

"The peoples of the world," he said softly, "are concerned with these things in the abstract, but mostly, we the people are willing to leave this to the theorists, while we rejoice.

"For we the people, who thought we faced that most degrading, that most unanswerable, that most horrible fate of all, bacteriological war, find ourselves at bacteriological peace."

At the break, the thirteen witches danced on, crying their chant, and behind them as a background was the bright, clean sub-and-shanty scene.

"Witches of the world unite, to make it clean, clean, clean, Witch clean—NOW!" they chanted. "Pestilence or peril, disease or disaster, Stay clean, clean, clean, Witch clean!"

"Ah," said the deep voice of the announcer as the jingle muted, "Which witch do you really wish? Witch is the modern method of cleanliness, using the best of modern technology, and the Witch which is witching through the world . . ."

Randolph watched the program skeptically. The best lawyers and the best p.r. agents to be had, he reminded himself. Still . . . There was a nagging worry that this thing was going too far. It's O.K. to claim the moon, he thought, chewing his lip, but isn't it a little risky to claim peace on earth for the Witch products?

He made a mental note to call BDD&O the next morning. The audience reaction would make itself felt by then, and he could decide . . .

It was almost noon next day before Randolph reminded himself of the call he'd planned to make to BDD&O. He got Oswald on the wire almost immediately.

"Randolph, here," he said. "I called about that new commercial. It seems a little drastic to claim peace on earth for the Witch products. What are you planning for tonight?"

"More of the same!" Oswald's voice was jubilant. "The switchboard has been swamped, and we're on almost every program on every channel! They're taking us apart, of course. 'Witchcraft raises its head,' and 'Salem is here with a new twist and a singing commercial,' and 'Anybody got a pestilence?'—that sort of thing. But they're crediting Witch products from dawn to dawn. I sure didn't make a mistake when I tied our contract to your sales! We ought to break the bank!"

Randolph chewed the thought in silence. "Oswald," he said, "it's an old habit of the American people to make a joke out of what they can't understand. Sort of Paul Bunyan all over again. But don't overdo it. That Witches of the world unite, deal. Remember the IWW? Wasn't that sort of communistic?"

"Every time anybody talks about getting the world peacefully together, about unity, somebody starts shouting 'commie.' Since when has communism and unity got anything to do with anything? You're an international corporation, aren't you? It's in your title, IWC, isn't it? You don't just sell Witch things in the United States—you've markets in Europe and Africa and India, and all over the place, or I read the sales charts wrong. What's worrying you about using it?

"The overseas tapes are going like a cannonball express. Our ratings have skyrocketed everywhere," Oswald said in satisfaction. "What do you mean, don't overdo it? You get the world in a hatbasket, and then you want to throw it away?

"Incidentally," he added in a calmer tone, "I got one crank call that's got me thinking. The guy got all the way through to me before he'd talk, and that takes some getting, what with the salaries I pay people to keep the cranks off my neck.

"He said that now we had the witches of the world united, why didn't we do some real clean up work, like slums and insane asylums. Got me thinking, you know. A good cause never did a program any harm."

Randolph chewed his lip a while in silence, and Oswald, knowing his client, waited patiently.

"I like that a lot better than claiming peace on earth for the Witch products," Randolph said at last. "Why don't you pick a slum we can clean up for not too much, and let's see what you can work out. This clean up theme isn't bad, it's just peace on earth that doesn't really belong to us you know.

"I tell you what. We'll go to fifty thousand dollars or so on a clean up job, and you use that. Leave the world to the politicians and the eggheads."

After he hung up, Randolph stood by the telephone, still chewing his lip. Could you clean up something like a slum for say fifty thousand dollars? Oswald would double the figure in his own mind, of course, always did. But he'd get the sales out of it. His contract was tied to sales.

Yes, he thought, it was best to call him off the track he was on now. Lawyers or no lawyers, that sort of thing was dangerous.

It took a week, and it took every member of the staff that could be pulled off other programs, as well as the ones assigned to Witch.

The "slum" had been located—three buildings in a short block just up from the Battery, surrounded by new buildings. It was a one-privy-to-a-floor, cold-water only setup, with a family living in every room. It existed on high-value land only because the land and buildings were tied up in an estate and couldn't be sold. But they could be remodeled and thrown into one, and contracts were signed, permissions granted, the paperwork alone filled nearly a complete file cabinet.

It would take double the fifty thousand dollars, of course —maybe more. But Randolph had authorized it, hadn't he? He always named half the figure—or less—than he meant to be used. Anyhow, international ratings and sales would more than make up the purse, because this thing would hit socko. Worry about the cash was the last thing that was bothering Oswald. He had a bear by the tail, and his contract price was tied to the gross . . .

The show was ballyhooed the whole week while the work went on.

"Clean, clean, Witch clean—what's the witches next big clean up? Witches of the world, unite—let's clean up this old world and make it livable . . ."

The night the new clean up job was to show, Randolph tuned in his TV as ignorant of the details as the next viewer. It worried him a little that Oswald insisted on keeping him in the dark on everything except the fact that it would be a slum clean up, but he had the best p.r. men and the best lawyers in the country working on it, he told himself; and certainly the sales charts for the past two weeks had been spectacular.

"We can count on the biggest TV audience of the year tonight," Oswald had told him gleefully at noon. "The buildup's been a natural, and those 'Salem with a new twist and a singing commercial' plugs have been continued on this network—the cost of that was comparatively small—and I've even gotten them onto a few of the really big shows to boot."

Bill Howard came on the screen, his big homely face leaning across the desk toward the TV audience.

"The biggest news in the country right now," Bill said in

a solemn tone, "is the biggest single clean up job in the country today.

"There's a slum," Bill said, "right here in New York that the Witches of the world will unite to clean up—tonight."

Then he put on the full power of the personality that made him the most listened-to newscaster on the air, TV and radio. The manner that made the news sound human, like it really happened to real people. He put it on full power, and went to work.

First he showed a big map of New York, and talked about how people thought of it as a big, impersonal place, but it wasn't. He made it everybody's home town.

Then he traced the map right down to the exact spot where the buildings were. Then he turned on a movie, and he showed the backdoor, garbage strewn, and a room where a family slept, seven of them, and the privy they shared with five other families.

Then Bill turned off the movie, and he brought that family to the mike, each of them dirty and in clothes that never had amounted to much, and had seen a long life since—even the baby. One kid's shoes had a sole flapping off, another had the toes cut out so he could wear them, though he'd long outgrown them.

"We haven't added to what we found," Bill said. "This is the way the . . . I've introduced them as the Jones family, let's leave it at that. This is how the Joneses have had to dress. This is how they've had to live. This is a very real part of America," he said, and his voice was choking a little, and Randolph thought, if he's putting that on, he's the best actor I've seen yet.

Randolph found himself glad he was alone, and didn't have to speak himself. His own throat felt choked.

"And now," said Bill to his audience, "It's time for the witches . . ."

The camera shifted, and there was a papier-mâché model of the buildings, built so you could look in the curtainless windows and see the squalor, lighted with a single bulb on a string. There was a gray pall over the whole thing, and newspapers and trash blowing against the front of the building. The gray pall, Randolph had figured from the sub-scene two weeks ago, was an effect of lights on a net curtain, but the effect was really good.

The thirteen witches, slender witches, danced in waving their products and crying their chant, their crimson-lined capes swirling out to glimpse the audience their long, slender legs.

They cried their chant as they pranced toward the dilapidated building. "Witches of the world, unite to make it clean, clean, clean, Witch clean—NOW!" And each threw a spray of her product toward the building.

"Witch soap or detergent, Witch cleanser upsurgent, which Witch do you need? You should have them all. . . ."

Then riding over the muted jingle the deep voice of the announcer saying "Tonight the Witches of the world clean a slum of the world . . . a particular slum, this slum.

"Witches, unite! And clean, clean, clean, Witch clean. . . ."

The dancing witches now threw each her ingredient on the building itself, and the gray pall began to lighten, a bright, new-painted front shone forth. Inside, the single bulbs blacked out for an instant, and then a soft light showed through curtained windows, a bright new scene dimly apparent through the curtains.

"This is not just an illusion," the deep voice of the announcer continued. "This is really happening, down near the Battery in New York City. It is happening to the Joneses and the Smiths who live there—"

The chorus rose to cover the announcer's voice, "Clean, clean, clean, Witch clean!"

The commercial and the witches faded, and Bill Howard's big, homely face came back on the screen.

"Let me introduce you again to the Jones family," Bill said. "I'll introduce you to the Joneses, but they're just one of the families who will now have a decent place to live— and the same miracle has happened to each of these families."

Now the Joneses came again on camera—clean, in new clothes, hair brushed, a miracle indeed of the costume-changers speedy art. Randolph assumed that teams of BDD&O members had been at work during the commercial, creating the miracle. From the baby up and down they shone, and their faces shone with an inner light—

When Randolph shut off the TV that night, he was chewing his lip violently. Must have been more than double that fifty thousand dollars, he thought. He reminded himself to phone BDD&O first thing in the morning.

It was still an hour before noon when Randolph's phone rang.

"Randolph, here," he said in the formality he'd adopted on an English visit and carefully kept.

"Good morning," Oswald's voice was formal. "Good morning." There was a silence, while Randolph waited for the other to continue.

Finally, Randolph said, "Good show, that. Must have cost a lot more than my price," he added. "It was good, though," he said again, thoughtfully.

"Randolph," Oswald's voice sounded wild, "I don't know what the thing cost. I don't know—"

"Now, sir, just what do you mean, you don't know the cost? I told you to spend fifty thousand dollars, and from what I saw last night it'll cost four times that. I'll go as high as one hundred twenty-five thousand dollars, but not one cent over. And you'd better make it worth the money, for that's a pretty penny," he said.

"Look, Randolph, the clean up job down there was supposed to start this morning. Contracts let, big crews ready to do the job fast so people could go look at the finished product. Every family was signed up to act as guides, like in Williamsburg. We moved 'em all to the country yesterday, so they'd look healthy when they came back, and the job could start at the crack of dawn today."

"Well?"

"Well, the job's already done."

"That's pretty fast. You said you started it this morning."

"Yeah. And when my man phoned me from down there I told him to get black coffee and sober up. But I went down myself—and the job's done. Exactly the job we specified, too. Done by our plans. Furnished, painted, paint dry, curtains hung, the works, new bathrooms and kitchen and plumbing and electricity. The works. It's finished.

"My best man was down there moving the families out yesterday. He swears the building hadn't been touched then. The contractor says he's going to sue, because he arrived with his crews to start the job, and somebody else had done it. You come on. You've got to meet me here and tell me the answers.

"Just what do you put in that soap of yours, anyhow?"

By afternoon it was banners in every paper, wire-serviced across the nation and the world.

Most of the stories were written tongue-in-cheek about the miracle part. It was assumed that Witch Products had done the inside job in advance, and thrown in the outside clean up during the night.

The tenants were interviewed—Oswald had the sense to move them right back into their new apartments—and not one of them could be made to break down and admit that those buildings hadn't been slums yesterday. Well, you couldn't blame them for sticking by Witch, look what Witch had done for them was the word that went around Bleek's.

Of course the thing was a curiosity natural, and the police had so many men assigned there by nightfall it looked like a concentration camp. TV portables and news photographer's flashbulbs didn't lessen the confusion any, and the crowds were being let in and through only when there was room for more.

Bill Howard was there when Randolph went through, in earnest conversation with a group of youngsters in one room. Oswald arranged that the Witch manufacturer should have a strong police escort, and the crowds moved back to make way for him in each apartment.

The tenants answered his questions, but they did so with a sullenness that surprised Randolph. Yes, it had been a mess the day before. Yes, it had been rebuilt, obviously, during the night, while they were gone. Yes, just the one night.

"They should be saying thank you," Randolph noted to Oswald. "They're acting as though I were a suspicious character."

"It's our escort," Oswald explained suavely. "These people don't think of cops as their friends. Besides, this is pretty new to them."

Randolph chewed his lip, and decided that Oswald was probably right. But the attitude was general, and it irritated him. He left after the briefest go-through.

That night Bill Howard was conservative in recounting the big news-story of the "slum clearance." He wasn't giving it the real Howard try, Randolph thought, sitting in front of his TV. There was a quote in the story he told, too, from the father of the Jones family that had been on the program the night before. "I reckon it's pretty wonderful, Mr. Howard," Jones had told him. "But I don't rightly know that I like it. Must admit I'm scared of this stuff," he had said, and he waved his hand at the newness.

It was just a single sour note in the story, but it stuck out. The rest was a description, without any mention of the "miracle" part.

At the break, the witches played the credit line to the hilt, though.

"Witches of the world unite to make it clean, clean, clean, Witch clean—NOW!" they chanted their cry, and re-enacted the scene of the night before, while the announcer's voice rode over the muted jingle to explain that Witch products had been used to make the slum clean, clean, Witch clean, even though it took carpenters and builders and contractors to remodel a slum building itself. That's better, thought Randolph, watching. No more of this "miracle" nonsense.

It was barely 10:00 A.M. next morning when Randolph's phone rang.

"Randolph, here," he said, and heard Oswald's voice without preliminary.

"They've gone."

"Who's gone?"

"The tenants of the building. Just picked up their duds and left. I've put dicks on the case, and one family has moved in with relatives in the Bronx. The others scattered, but we'll trace 'em. Here's one of the policemen that was on duty when they left. He'll tell you."

A new voice came on the phone, as Randolph chewed his lip.

"Mr. Randolph? This is what happened, near as I can figure. We roped off the area at dark, last night. Figured we'd give the families some rest, and keep out the night-thrill guys.

"Everybody in the apartments must have gotten together after we cleared out the crowds. It was pretty quiet, but the lights stayed on till about 2:00 A.M. Then they all started parading out, some even wearing their old clothes. They were carrying a few things, but nothing that looked like they hadn't had it before the change, so we figured what they were taking was theirs, probably.

"Didn't say a word. Just paraded past us. Some of the kids was crying, but otherwise they were quiet."

"Then one man came running back to me, and he said 'Get out of here. It's the devil's work. Get away from this place if you're a God-fearing man.' Then he turned and ran toward the subway with the rest.

"I couldn't figure we had any orders to stop 'em, so we didn't try. We just watched."

Oswald came back on the phone.

"Can you keep it out of the papers?" Randolph asked.

"It's already on every newscast, and the papers'll have it by noon—it's on the wires," Oswald said.

Randolph coughed nervously, but Oswald didn't wait for him to speak.

"I'm working on something to counteract this," he said.

"We're being witch-hunted," Oswald said. "I'll get the whole firm to work on it and call you back."

In Washington, meantime, another conference was going on, far more intent, far more critical.

"It's more than just a pest plane that crashed in Formosa, Mr. President," the CIA chief was saying. "It carried bacterial bombs, and they exploded.

"There's been no attempt to hide its source. It's, of course, of enemy make. No identification on the bodies aboard, they're in civilian clothes. But again, the make is Moscow.

"It shouldn't be long before we know the worst."

"Will they clean this one up as they did the last one, or will they demand surrender terms on this one?" the President asked.

The Secretary of State and the Secretary of War started to answer together, but it was State that got the first word in.

"I think they'll clean this one up," he said. "It would be a direct threat on which they'll demand surrender terms. That's just a guess, of course.

"The best teams of doctors are being organized and jetted over. The best bacteriologists the nation has at its command. Every antibiotic available is being sent."

"Will that make a dent?"

"No."

"How long can we keep it under wraps?"

"A week. Ten days, perhaps, with top security."

"Give it everything you've got. But keep it quiet until we know what the next move is. Twenty-four hour alert, of course, immediately."

"Even if the alert itself endangers the security wraps?"

"Yes. A week to ten days of security isn't enough to pay for taking a chance the other way."

By 4:00 P.M. Oswald was on the phone to Randolph. "We've got the antidote," he said jubilantly.

Randolph was quiet for a minute, chewing his lip. Then: "I'm being vilified in the press as the creator of a hoax that even those who stood to benefit by it couldn't take," he said. "The few who have decided that a real miracle occurred have also decided that I'm in league with the devil, and that witches are for burning. Mostly Witch is the butt of every joke that can be dreamed up by every cub reporter in the nation. Saxton has started laying the groundwork for making Witch a political issue. There is talk of an FCC investigation.

"I trust," he said formally, "that your antidote is an efficient one."

Oswald's voice sounded smug, and not at all disgruntled. "Try this on for size," he said. "First, Witch is known far and wide as nothing less could have made it known—"

"Yes, and if the churches ban the use of Witch, we'll wish we weren't."

"O.K., O.K. Tonight we explain carefully that the 'miracle' was a miracle of cleanliness, and that carpenters and contractors and all that did the miracle. You know, American technology and mass production in operation, something to be proud of. Tie Witch right in to the whole picture of the United States as the leader of mechanical—stress mechanical—miracles.

"Then—what's the most appealing thing in the world?" He didn't wait for an answer. "A child. A small, crippled child, for whom Witch can provide the funds to make her walk." Oswald hurried on, knowing that Randolph had to go through a bit of lip chewing before he could interrupt, and taking advantage of the fact to ride over objections.

"We've got a kid that an expensive operation will save from being a cripple. I've consulted two top surgeons already, and they say it's nearly positive.

"We don't do any hocus-pocus. We just say that Witch is going to pay for the operation. She leaves the broadcast and goes straight to the hospital. We get a movie of the operation, and we do movies on her convalescence, and we play it for weeks until she walks on stage cured—weeks later."

Now Oswald waited. It was a long wait, an unusually long wait, even for Randolph. Finally, he said:

"All right. But if anything unusual occurs you will answer for it in court."

"Nothing unusual could occur. I admit I still don't know what happened last time, but we'll find out.

"Meantime, we'll take a week to build this one up," Oswald continued. "The buildup will stress that this is a cure being bought by money. No miracle, except the miracle of American medical know-how. No miracles meantime. Just keep Witch clean and stay well, and Witch buys the operation the kid needs. She's pretty, too," he added as an after-thought. "Ten years old."

That night Bill Howard leaned across the desk toward the TV audience, and tiny droplets of sweat stood on his fore-head. His voice was calm, though. A big map of New York City hung on the wall behind him.

The big news that night was a dope raid. He described the dope traffic in the nation, the efforts of the FBI and every law enforcement body in the country, to track it down, clean it out. He described what it did to the young, who got caught and were slaves for life, unless they could be cured—and he spoke of the meagerness of the cures that were known.

Then he described the raid. He took a pointer from his desk and he outlined how the raid had been staged, and he pointed out the location of the building where it had oc-curred. Then he followed with his pointer the route to the precinct jail where the victims were being held.

"Cannot our best researchers find a cure for this addic-tion?" he asked in his husky voice. "Cannot our best law-enforcement agencies find the real perpetrators of these crimes? The perpetrators are the fiends who import dope and create addicts to peddle it for them. These who are confined are the victims. If no way can be found to cure them, they must be confined again and again and again, for that addiction will force them to ever-increasing crime to satisfy it.

"If no way can be found to cure them, these are potential slaves for life—"

As he ended the station break came, and the camera shifted to the Witches, dancing on stage, crying their chant.

"Witches of the world, unite to make it clean, clean, clean, Witch clean—NOW!

"Witch soap or detergent, Witch cleanser upsurgent—"

The announcer's voice, when it came in over the muted jingle "explained" the miracle of the slum-clearance again —a miracle of American technology. Then he outlined the next "miracle" the Witch Corporation would promote. This, he said, would be a miracle of American medical know-how. Witch would pay for the expensive operation needed to make a little girl walk again after a crippling disease several years before. Bone would be grafted, new muscles would be grafted, American medical know-how in its full extent would be put at her service.

Keep healthy by keeping clean with Witch, the announcer suggested. Witch would pay for the expensive operation to undo the effects of one disease. Meanwhile, Witch's customers could use the preventive medicine of cleanliness to help them in their fight against disease, while the researchers of American medicine "seek to find you real protection."

It was 10:30 the next morning when the doorbell rang.

A big man was standing outside in a topcoat, hat in hand. Randolph stood in the door, waiting.

The man silently held out a badge, and Randolph moved aside, gesturing him in.

"I didn't look at your badge close enough," Randolph said as he closed the door behind his visitor. "Who are you?"

"Narcotics squad," the man said briefly. "I was on the raid last night."

"Oh? The one Bill Howard was talking about in his newscast?"

"Yes. That one. I don't figure there's any connection, and my boss just laughed when I suggested there was a connection."

"Connection?"

"You see, I took a break from questioning those boys we pulled in. Trying to get a lead to the higher-ups. They were doped to the ears, and sometimes you can get info from them right quick. I took a break for a cup of coffee across the street, and there was a TV in the place, and I watched your Bill Howard.

"I left just when your witches came on, shouting that thing about make it clean NOW. I went right back and started in on the questioning again, but the guy they brought in for me to question next was—not dopey. He was . . . well, there's a difference between boys with the monkey on their back, and when there's no monkey. There was no monkey, but the kid began giving me everything he knew would take us to the higher-ups. It was being taped, of course, and I asked him when he'd had his last shot. Not twenty minutes before the raid, he said, calm as you please.

"I had the guys brought back that I'd talked to before and they were—different. Only way I can describe it is, no monkey. The monkey had been there before. I don't know. They each gave us all they had in leads—they'd been stubborn before, but they sang like canaries.

"I checked and nobody'd done anything to 'em to bring 'em off their jazz. If there's anything can be done to pull a guy out of a jazz, anyhow, I've never heard of it, and I've been in the narcotics squad since the year One. I couldn't figure it. I'd been hearing stories about Witch products and that miracle at the Battery, sort of as a joke, and I thought, just maybe, just possibly, you know . . .

"Anyhow, I took the tapes to my boss, and spoke my bit, but he just laughed.

"Maybe you'll just laugh, too, but I thought I'd ask."

At the same time in Washington, the cabinet was in full session. Reports coming in from Formosa were worse than even the most pessimistic had dreamed. The bacteria hit at the nerves and the brain, and the victims—excruciating was a word being used.

"It's hit everywhere on the island at once. I assume it is contagious as well as having been broadcast from whatever bombs or broadcast methods were used," the CIA chief reported.

"Any word from their embassy?"

State answered that one. "No word at all. Phone calls to the Ambassador only elicit reports that he is not available. I can't reach anybody higher than a fourth assistant under-secretary."

"At least it's not been on the air or in the press."

"I don't know how long we can hold them in leash. Most of your leading papers know there's a twenty-four hour alert on—that was bound to leak—but I've kept them quiet. We'll have to give them something soon, though. They won't take a muzzle too long without at least knowing why."

"Could you give them the story and trust them, when it's this important, and the consequences of leakage this apparent?"

"I'd thought of that. You can convince some newsmen— but there's always a Joe somewhere who figures the American people have a right to know their destiny before it's decided, no matter what the effect—and no matter if their most highly elected officials feel it would not be good for them."

"Keep it top security as long as possible. Let me know before it breaks."

"If I can. I'm not a witch. I might not know when it was breaking." The CIA chief grinned sourly at his own allusion.

The next night, the big news was the countdown in process at Canaveral to put a functioning "dome" on the moon. If the dome could be landed successfully, complete with live animals, a man would follow shortly. That was foregone. The question was landing the dome, just a small spaceship body, but completely equipped to keep a man alive for two years, in case anything went wrong with plans to bring him back pronto.

Bill Howard's voice was excited, and he ran his fingers through his hair, pushing it back as he leaned across the desk, the map of Florida behind him.

"To the statesmen, this is a question of who is first and who is second, and perhaps who will control the spaceways," he said after describing the countdown in process.

"But to the peoples of the world, this is mankind, reaching for the stars.

"It is not known," he said solemnly, "whether the failure of many of our shots has been human error or sabotage. Human error is a frailty of the race. Sabotage is a frailty of statemenship, that the world is still divided as it reaches for the stars. Yet each is possible.

"Is there a mechanical error built in by human frailty in tonight's shot? Is there a saboteur at work?

"Or, as the countdown reaches zero, one hour from now, will the dome tear through the atmosphere of Earth in man's first real step to the stars successfully? Is our bird perfect this time?" he asked, as the break came.

The witches danced on crying their chant . . . "Witches of the world, unite to make it clean, clean, clean, Witch clean,—NOW!"

Randolph was chewing his lip still as he went to bed that night. The man from the Narcotics Squad had left peaceably. There were answers to all the questions, and it wasn't his worry anyway. He'd be glad when the little girl had her operation. Grafting bones and muscles might be miraculous, but they were explicable and everybody understood them. Talk of the FCC investigation had died aborning, but talk like that was enough to upset anybody. Everything had been upsetting recently, even though the up-curve on Witch products was holding steady.

The American dome landed on the moon the morning of the day that the crippled child was scheduled to come on the Witch program.

For the American people it was a day of celebration comparable to the Fourth of July. In the White House gloom hung like a palpable shroud.

"They'll have to move fast now," the Secretary of War was reporting to his chief. "They can't afford to let us get our man up there. Even if we could shoot him off successfully."

"We can't shoot a man up there until we've proved in at least two more successful shots that we can get him there," Security declared forcefully. "The threat from our enemies is as nothing to the threat from the vote-wielding public if we tried and failed when a human life is at stake."

"Formosa is leaking," admitted the CIA chief. "We can't hold it more than three days now at the outside."

The President rested a hand on his desk. "Two more shots mean at least six months before a man is up there, armed. Three days means Formosa is in the news this week. When the news breaks, credit our doctors and bacteriologists with being on the way to a cure. Fix it so that if they clean up their epidemic, the way they did Suez, we get the credit.

"That's the best we can do right now. Besides looking for a miracle. But miracles are popular these days," he added ruefully.

It was Bill Howard who stood outside when Randolph answered his doorbell next morning. He let the big, homely, almost shambling figure in without a word.

"I came to ask you a question I don't think you can answer," Howard said morosely, not moving farther than the foyer.

"I came to ask you what it is about the witches?"

Randolph chewed his lip, standing there beside his much-larger guest, conscious of his own prim—almost prissy—neatness as it contrasted to the other's shaggy look. Shaggy dog, thought Randolph. Big, unkempt, shaggy St. Bernard.

"What about the witches?" he asked finally.

"Well . . . there have been some funny things. That slum, of course. I was there, of course. I saw it. And I talked to the small-fry. It was a tenement the day before, I'd stake a lot on it."

There was a silence before Randolph answered.

"Well?"

"Well, then a few little things. A narcotics man came to

see me. Just personal. Just curious. They've been pulling in the higher-ups in the dope traffic, by the way—on info from the guys caught in that raid.

"Then that Canaveral deal? Were you listening that night?"

"I always tune you in. It seems to me that today is one of celebration. The dome landed."

"Yeah. Yeah, celebration. I'm a newsman, and I get stories that don't go out. There's one that just an hour before zero—a man suddenly died of a heart attack. The technician who took his place—you don't stop a countdown like that for a heart attack—checked his work and found an error that would have misfired the thing. There was also one circuit that had been changed, but they left that because it was changed to be more accurate. They figured the dead guy had done it."

"So?"

"So . . . well, nothing. I just wanted to ask you. The witches don't touch anything real these days, of course, so even if . . . they were . . . well, magic somehow, they couldn't have been involved."

There wasn't even a pause for lip-chewing this time.

"Are you trying to insinuate that Witch products—"

The question was left hanging, but Bill Howard stood looking his sponsor in the eye.

"Mr. Randolph, I'm not trying to insinuate one damn thing. I'm not even saying anything to anybody, and if I did say anything I'd be laughed off the air, not by you, but by whoever I said it to.

"I'm just telling you what twos and twos have been setting themselves in front of my everlasting consciousness, and asking if you know anything to add to them?"

The lip-chewing started again, and the two stood there. Then Randolph said quietly, "Mr. Howard, I have been manufacturing Witch products for twenty-five years. They have been improved steadily since I first started with a very good formula. They are the best cleaning products available in the world today, I most sincerely believe. They are that exactly, and nothing more than that exactly. So you will have to find another explanation for your twos and twos, which I admit are a rather spectacular run of coincidence, though not beyond the bounds of credibility.

"Myself, I suspect BDD&O with perpetrating some sort of hoax in the first instance. If any more hoaxes are perpetrated, I plan to switch agencies, switch programs, and call for an FCC investigation of BDD&O to clear the Witch name, which never has and never would condone any hoax of any sort, much less one of the magnitude of whatever occurred, which I profess I do not understand, but which I expect the FCC can trace to its source.

"Good day to you, sir." Randolph ended the unprecedentedly long speech, turned on his heel and left Bill Howard to find his own way out.

That night, as Bill Howard ended his newscast, the camera did not switch to the witches. Instead it switched to the announcer.

"Tonight, Witch products would like you to meet a little girl," the announcer said in a soft voice that contrasted well with Howard's just ended powerful one.

As he spoke the camera backed away to broaden its scope and include in its picture, beside the announcer, a small blond child in a wheel chair. Her hair was shoulder-length and carefully combed. Her eyes were downcast shyly. Her hands gripped the arms of the wheel chair as though for security. Her legs were covered with a shawl.

"This is Mary," said the announcer, then leaned toward her. "Will you speak to the audience, Mary?"

She lifted deep blue eyes briefly to the camera, then dropped them quickly. "Hello," she said in a voice barely audible.

"Mary is not used to many people, or to audiences," the announcer said. "Mary has been sitting in this wheel chair for almost three years, since a crippling disease twisted her limbs.

"We hope that Mary can be made to walk. The finest surgeons in the country have been consulted, and they believe an operation can give her back her legs, that were twisted when the disease struck. International Witch Corporation has arranged for that operation.

"Tomorrow Mary will go to the hospital. She will have the operation soon. In a few weeks, perhaps Mary will walk.

"Will you like that, Mary? Will you like walking?" he asked, leaning toward the child.

Again the eyes lifted for the briefest instant. Again they dropped shyly.

"Yes," Mary said in that barely audible voice.

"Then you shall have it, if it can be done," the announcer said, and the camera moved even farther back to include a stage onto which the witches danced.

The witches came onto the stage, not toward Mary, but stage center, chanting—their cry.

"Witches of the world, unite to make it clean, clean, clean, Witch clean,—NOW!"

At the corner of the screen, the child-body in the wheel chair shuddered suddenly. Mary took a deep breath, went white and then red. With a forceful gesture she threw off the shawl and looked at her legs. Her hand reached down to touch them.

On the stage itself, one witch stopped dancing to watch. The others noticed, stopped. The jingle died, half through . . .

And Mary stood up, looking at her legs. She took a step towards the camera, and another. Her blue eyes lifted to the camera, widening.

In the absolute quiet, as everyone on stage stood frozen, Mary walked towards the camera, her eyes like saucers looking into it. Her voice, barely above a whisper, spoke.

"I'm . . . I'm walking," said Mary.

The papers called it the cruelest hoax of all.

They carried the story side by side with the withdrawal of the Witch program from the network, both by network and by International Witch Corporation order.

They carried the statement of FCC officials that an investigation would be made.

They carried the statement by Randolph that he would sue BDD&O.

They carried the statement by Oswald that he would sue Witch products.

But mostly they carried the story of a little girl, who had been whisked from sight and couldn't be located. Who had probably been given an operation to make it possible for her to walk, but had been forced to pay for the operation by taking part in a cruel hoax of unbelievable magnitude.

Bill Howard stayed with the network, on the same time, sponsorless. He'd been cleared of any implication in the hoax by all parties concerned, and his reputation had always been good. He was asked to stay in town and be available to appear as a witness, but the network gambled that he was clear, and kept him on. He was one of the biggest draws in newscasting, his personality that made the news seem to belong to the people, to be a continuing story of their lives, was unique. The network decided the gamble of keeping him on was warranted.

By the next night the Formosa crisis had broken into the news, and it was the news.

The details were horrible, and they were uncovered aplenty. Finally ungagged, those who had been holding off gave the story the works.

The effects of the pest plane, of the pest bombs, were the most vicious that could be developed in the laboratories of bacterial war—and they put to shame the naturally-occurring epidemics that have scourged mankind throughout his history.

And the effects were spreading with the speed of a prairie fire before a high wind.

The entire area was quarantined, and daily the quarantine was extended. No plane could land and take off again. No ship could enter and leave. An airlift of supplies dropped by parachute was being organized.

Bacteriologists and doctors jetted to the area were dying with the rest, caught in disease for which there was no answer.

The propaganda attempts to make it seem as though cures were near were flatly not believed. Suez was remembered, but was remembered as a hoax—and the country had had its complete fill of hoaxes.

Randolph had a number of what he referred to—and

reported—as "crank calls," asking Witch to try its might. He arranged for every call that reached him to be traced immediately. He remained in seclusion.

Oswald had a few of the "crank calls" and reported them as such.

Bill Howard had a number of calls, and didn't report them.

Bill Howard worried, and added two and two, and sweated, and reported the details of Formosa each night. The details giantized in gruesomeness until their very content was too much for the airways, and he had to censor them as he gave them out.

Bill Howard sweated in the cold January weather, and each day he ferreted further, seeking out the realities behind the censorship that lay heavy now even over the wires. By phone, by gossip, by hearsay and by knowhow he got the stories behind the story—the real horrors that he couldn't broadcast.

Sometimes he rebelled at the censors and himself as one of them, but he knew better than to rebel. It's facing us all, he thought. We each have the right to know.

This is the way the world ends, he thought. With a whimper that comes after the agony, when agony is too great.

And he kept remembering a little girl walking towards a camera with big eyes.

If I were a physicist, he told himself, if I were a physicist instead of a newshawk, I could get a computer to tell me the probability ratio of whether I hold an answer.

That probability ratio is probable ten billion to one, he told himself.

That probability ratio is zero.

Witches are for burning, he told himself.

He told himself a lot of things, and he sweated through the cold January weather.

It had been two weeks since the world heard the first details of Formosa, and the details were so grim now that you couldn't use them at all. Just a blanket story.

That night, the map of the world behind his desk, Bill Howard leaned toward his audience.

He told them the human side of the story of Formosa.

He spoke of the people there, the pawns in a game of international suicide, real people, not just statistics.

He described a family, and he made them the family next door. Mother, father, children, watching one another die, not prettily but with all the torture that the laboratories of the world could dream and put together. A family that watched each other go insane, knowing what was happening. A family that watched each other die, writhing and unknowing in insanity.

He took his pointer and he showed the growing perimeter of the quarantine. He traced the location of the center of the disaster.

Then he leaned again toward his audience. "Listen, now," he said, "for the world cannot sustain this torture."

He took a deep breath and he put the full force of his being into his words.

"Witches of the world, unite," he said, "to make it clean, clean, clean, Witch clean—NOW!"

The final word was out before the network censor reached the cut-off switch.

The President and his cabinet put the country on a double alert. Russia had cleaned up Formosa, they knew, and would hit the United States with disease and ultimatums next.

The people of the world took the story with an unexpected calm. Like Hiroshima, it was too unexpected, too big, too unimaginable. There was a hooker somewhere, and they went about their business annoyed, angry, worried, but quiet.

The papers editorialized on the question of who cleaned up Formosa—who had the answers?—and left the subject of what the possession of such a clean-up force could mean to the world, to the statesmen. They turned as quickly as possible to other matters, for nobody was sure what to think, and nobody told them what to think.

Bill Howard was off the air, of course. It didn't bother him. He had a real problem now.

We've bought a little time, he thought. A little time to grow in.

We've bought a little time from the fanatics and their statesmen, from the eggheads and their politicians, from the military and the industrial and the just generally foolhardy.

We, the people of the world, have a little time now that we didn't have yesterday.

How much? He didn't know.

On this one, there'd been time to get together. On this one, there'd been weeks, while the crisis built and the world faced a horrible death. This crisis had been a lengthy one. There'd been time for a man to make up his mind and try a solution.

The next one might be different. There might be a satellite up there waiting, with a button to be pushed. There were an awful lot of buttons waiting to be pushed, he told himself, buttons all over the world, controlling missiles already zeroed in on—well, on the people of the world.

The next one might occur in hours, or even minutes. The next one, the bombs might be in the air before the people even knew the buttons were for pushing.

Bill Howard got out his typewriter.

You've got a problem, you talk to a typewriter, if that's the only thing that will listen.

What's the problem? he asked himself, and he wrote it down. He started at the beginning and he told the story on the typewriter. He told it the way it had been happening.

Now, he thought, you've got to end the story. If you leave it just "to be continued," it'll be continued, all right. Somebody will push a button one day, and that will write 30 at the end for you. Conclusion.

The problem was, in essence, quite simply stated in terms of miracles.

The way things were stewing, it'd be a miracle if the world held together long enough for unity to set in. It'd take a miracle to bring about the necessary self-restraint, which was the only possible substitute for the imposed restraint of war.

The witch power was, quite clearly, a power of the people—of the people who needed that protection, needed those miracles. And it was the power that had worked miracles.

We'll never know who does the job, he told himself. It's better that way. Like table-tipping. You can say "I didn't do it." You can even be sure you didn't do it, if you want to. But the table tips if you get enough people around the table. Ouija writes, if at least two people have their fingers on it, so that each can say "I didn't do it."

Who are the witches? Why, they're the people, and they're not for burning. The fanatics and their statesmen, the eggheads and their politicians, the brains and the brain trusts and the world-weary—they're for burning, but not the witches. Which witch is a witch? Doesn't matter.

An hour later, Bill Howard sat down to the typewriter again. He'd stated the general problem—but now he had a specific problem, and, for a man in his line of business, it was a fairly straightforward problem.

He need only plot out the necessary moves so that he could call on that witch power just one more time. Just once. Just long enough to clean out the violent, rooted resistance to the idea that people had powers—and could work miracles!